GOD BLESS AMERICA

Stories

GOD BLESS AMERICA

Stories

Steve Almond

LOOKOUT BOOKS

University of North Carolina Wilmington

©2011 Steve Almond

First printing, October 2011
ISBN: 978-0-9845922-3-4

Cover illustration by Valero Doval
Book design by Arianne Beros, Meg Reid, and Anna Sutton
for The Publishing Laboratory

These stories originally appeared, sometimes in different form, in the following publications: "Hagar's Sons" in *Ecotone*; "A Jew Berserk on Christmas Eve" in *Nerve* and the *Pisgah Review*; "A Dream of Sleep," "First Date Back," and "Shotgun Wedding" in *New England Review*; "Not Until You Say Yes" in *Ninth Letter*; "Akedah," "The Darkness Together," "God Bless America," and "What the Bird Says" in *Southern Review*; "Hope Wood" in *The Sun*; "Donkey Greedy, Donkey Gets Punched" in *Tin House*; "Tamalpais" in *Virginia Quarterly Review*.

"Donkey Greedy, Donkey Gets Punched" was selected for *Best American Short Stories* in 2010. "The Darkness Together" was included in *The Pushcart Prize* in 2006.

LIBRARY OF CONGRESS CATALOGING-IN-PUBLICATION DATA

Almond, Steve.
  God Bless America: Stories / Steve Almond.
    p. cm.
  ISBN 978-0-9845922-3-4
  I. Title.
  PS3601.L58G63 2011
  813'.6—dc22

             2011010332

Lookout Books gratefully acknowledges support from the University of North Carolina Wilmington, the North Carolina Arts Council, and the National Endowment for the Arts.

ART WORKS.
arts.gov

www.ncarts.org

LOOKOUT BOOKS
Department of Creative Writing
University of North Carolina Wilmington
601 South College Road
Wilmington, North Carolina 28403
www.lookout.org

for ERIN

CONTENTS

America is a passionate idea or it is nothing.
America is a human brotherhood or it is chaos.

—MAX LERNER

GOD BLESS AMERICA

Don't be extras. Be a nation!
—Cecil B. DeMille

BILLY CLAMM HAD NOT SIGNED UP FOR DRAMA I, he had signed up for a tax-preparation course called Loopholes Ahoy! But the Medford Adult Education facility was a confusing one, full of strange underground corridors and bunkers, and Billy was somewhat easily disoriented, somewhat prone to distraction, particularly during the bleak winter months, and so he had found his way to the wrong classroom.

The instructor, Mr. Denzel Hamish, was a short man who leaped a lot and kept tearing off his beret and twirling it on his index finger, and really the only reason Billy Clamm hadn't left the room—because it certainly didn't seem to him that a tax-preparation instructor should be wearing a beret—was because of the way Mr. Hamish spoke, as if his words had been coated in something very bright and echoey. "Are you *connected*?" he asked the seven assembled students. "Are any of you even the least bit *connected* to your own lives? Or do you have a sense of drifting? Drifting through this one and only life of yours, dodging the slings and arrows of outlandish fortune? Do you feel a certain emptiness is what I'm asking, a certain void that calls out at night to be filled?"

Billy, standing at the back of the room, allowed to slip from his hand his pop's Medford Credit Union promotional calculator.

"What I can offer you over the next eight weeks is a singular place, a haven, where you can finally start to *connect* to your lives. That place, ladies and gentlemen, is . . . *the stage*." With this, Mr. Hamish launched himself onto a box at the front of the room and cried, "Have we got trouble? Yes, sir, we do! Right here in River City!" And then began singing a song, quite loudly for a man his size, that involved the naming of numerous musical instruments, in particular trombones.

Over the next two months of class, Mr. Hamish introduced a variety of topics, sometimes, though not always, with a slight British accent. He addressed the importance of living *moment to moment* and calling out to the *artistic unconscious* and remaining *connected to your process*. In this way, Billy Clamm began to see himself in a new light.

His pop had often joshingly called him a "useless little poke." But Billy saw now that his supposed underachievement was a function of his disconnectedness and not a deficient attention span, as one or more of his teachers had implied. It was only a matter of hitching his wagon to the right dream; this was how his mother had phrased it. Now that he had done this, his life assumed a new urgency, not just on Tuesday nights, when classes were, but the entire week. He saw, for instance, that his job stocking at the Osco Pharmacy on Locust was a dead end creatively. That was why he had quit and not, as Pop was insisting, because he was "allergic to an honest day's labor." He spent a lot of time at the park off Winthrop Square watching passersby, studying their movements and privately mimicking them, *finding the character*, as Mr. Hamish put it. At night he watched black-and-white classics on cable.

This was how he prepped for class. Not that you could prep for improvisational exercises. No, you just had to let those happen and not *deny*, which he never did, even if sometimes his fellow students didn't understand what he was getting at, that he was enacting the near death of Red Sox legend Tony Conigliaro at the precise moment his eye socket was shattered by a fastball and not, as was the general consensus of the class, suffering a grand mal seizure. Mr. Hamish understood his aims perfectly, and that was why he sometimes took Billy aside and made comments such as "You are an ambitious student," and "Perhaps you should let your creative engine cool a bit." He was trying to communicate with Billy, speaking one actor to another, which was what Billy was, he realized, an *actor*, even before the final class, where he delivered the big Willy Loman speech from *Death of a Salesman*, the whole time thinking about his pop and how he banged around their apartment, so much so that he even began to improv a few lines in Pop's own voice, such as "What am I, the world's dishrag?" and "Who told you to get born?" and Billy was fairly certain that some of his classmates had teared up, though he couldn't be sure because he was *in character*. This performance, the feeling of destiny it inspired, was why Billy had begun describing his unemployment benefits as a kind of "grant."

He was not fooling himself. He knew the odds were stacked against him. He was thirty-five years old, for one thing, and not quite five and a half feet tall, and he was losing hair in clumps, and when he got nervous, which was nearly every time he did a scene, a blotch rose on his left cheek that made it look as if he had been scalded, though Billy felt confident this last defect could eventually be turned to his advantage, like Clark Gable's ears, or the way Katharine Hepburn's head shook around. Also, he had never acted before.

Still, there were plenty of actors who came to the field late, such as Robert Duvall, who hadn't landed a decent role until he was practically forty, and plenty of actors who were on the short side (Hoffman, DeVito) or bald (Malkovich, Brynner, Duvall—again!). Most good actors were either short or bald, when you actually did the math, because that kind of adversity forced a person to develop other parts of his personality, which is what Billy Clamm had been doing.

Ma would have understood. She was the one who had believed in him, who had insisted, time and again, that he could be anything he wanted, never mind Pop and his dark muttering. It would be two years in August since her passing, but Billy still felt her sometimes, watching over him, her mouth hitched up in that gentle smile as he ran his lines with her sewing dummy.

Billy was in Medford for the moment and that was good because it gave him an element of regional identity. But pretty soon, once he got a little cash socked away, he'd move out of Pop's place and head down to New York to check out that scene, the off-Broadway scene, but not out to LA, because as Mr. Hamish assured him, it was all about image out there, and not about integrity of process: *connectedness.*

This was why he'd signed on with Sammy Duck Land and Sea Tours, because there had been an ad in the *Herald* under the column "Actors Wanted," with an address in the North End. The man who answered the door said, "You got something for me?"

Billy said, "I brought my résumé."

The man, whose cheeks looked as if they had been scooped up with a trowel and then patted down again, said: "No funny stuff." Then he placed his hand on the butt of what appeared to be a gun jammed into the side of his waistband. Billy's pulse thumped and the room grew damp and he tried to explain, without actually speaking, that he was here about the classified ad. He held out his résumé.

"Oh," the man said. He removed his hand from the apparent gun butt and drew his coat around him like a cape and led

Billy into a smaller room, which Billy could not help but notice included a toilet and a sink. The man glanced down at the résumé. "William Clamm, huh? Ever done any work as a tour guide, William?"

Billy tried to focus on the question. But he was taken with the sound of his name, William, and how it rolled off the thick tongue of his interviewer. William Clamm. Names were an important part of the business. Although it occurred to Billy that he might want to do some work on that last name. William Clammato. William Clammentine. *Something.* "I was under the impression this was an acting job," he said finally.

"What it is, we got this tour. You go around to these sites downtown and also the harbor—that's what you call the sea portion of the tour—explaining about history." The man opened a desk drawer and handed Billy a pamphlet that showed a large red vehicle shaped like a hot dog bun, with cage-like window slots. Tourists were peering through the bars. The man driving the hot dog bun was outfitted in a red-and-white striped shirt and silver pantaloons and boots and something like an eye patch. He was smiling deliriously.

"You ever been arrested?" the man said.

"Arrested?" Billy said.

"*Fine,*" the man said. "I don't want to know." Then he shook Billy's hand and embarked on a brief orientation, which involved Billy's signing many non-indemnity forms, and during which Billy learned other important facts, such as that the man interviewing him was not Sam, but Augustino, and that Sam was an older gentleman who started the business years ago but was now legally in a "vegetative state" and that he (Billy) should never ever discuss method of payment and that Augustino did not carry a firearm, but if he did it was for security reasons only, because the neighborhood was full of young punks who didn't understand basic concepts like "respect" and had, on occasion, to be taught.

Heading out of the building on that chilly March day, with his uniform slung rakishly over his shoulder, Billy wandered down to the docks and watched the barges drifting in and the gantry cranes looming in the white mist and he thought about Brando and how Brando could have been a contender, how his brother, Joey, or perhaps Jimmy, should have helped him out, how some opportunities rise up and pass us by, and how, in the end, we have to create our own opportunities and not necessarily wait for our brother to rescue us; and this had special resonance for Billy, even though he did not have any brothers, only a mildly epileptic cousin who lived in Saugus.

Being a Sammy Duck tour guide was not technically an acting job, but it had elements of the craft, such as speaking before a captive audience, and interacting with the other guides at red lights, when they were supposed to perform little skits. There was also a reenactment of the Boston Tea Party, which was held at the end of the tour, near the harbor, and was clearly the dramatic highlight of the day. A Tea Party role was something you worked your way up to, in other words, a first step that would lead to more ambitious steps, such as clown gigs, dinner theater, and eventually commercial work. What was most important was your process, remaining *connected to your process*, and not worrying about the external measures of success, such as whether you had enough money to pay off your Discover card balance.

Traffic was difficult to negotiate in a Duckmobile. They cornered poorly. Then, too, there was the microphone clamp, which dug into the side of Bully's skull and caused tension headaches, and his costume, which Pop claimed made him look like a homosexual pirate. But these were small matters. Within a couple of months Billy had memorized the script and even begun to go *off script* when he felt this would be a lucrative artistic decision.

So that now, for instance, as the Duckmobile barreled down Boylston, with the Common yellow-green under the rippling June air, Billy flicked on his microphone and said: "Quack! Quack! To your left, Duckies, is the famous Boston Common.

In days of yore, cows were led to graze here. Its bucolic wonders inspired many of Ralph Waldo Emerson's essays, as well as a little-known skirmish during the War of Independence, the Battle of the Lawn. What do you think about that?"

From in back Billy heard a group of child Duckies burping in unison, which wasn't a thought, technically, but did reflect a spirit of improvisation.

"Quack! Quack! We are now entering Beacon Hill. This stately neighborhood of redbrick and cobbled streets was the original home to Boston's aristocracy! It is named after Ebenezer Beacon, who, coincidentally, is the same person who inspired Charles Dickens to write the novel *Ebenezer Scrooge*. He was a stingy grocer who would not allow poor families to borrow against his larder until he had a vision of God. He then wrote the song 'Amazing Grace,' which many black churches sing to this day."

Further along in life, when he penned his memoirs, Billy would look back on these days fondly, as an era full of the material necessary to the actor's craft. He was not one of those stars who had made it too easy, thank God, and spent his life behind a wall of security personnel. He was more like a young Brando, who learned his parts by spending time among stevedores and roustabouts and other interestingly named laborers. At night Billy would return home and stand before the mirror in his room, practicing accents. Pop was suspicious of this and banged on the door and sometimes threatened to throw Billy's clothing out into the street. This was his way of working through some unresolved issues.

Billy pulled up to a red light, next to another Duckmobile. He gave his horn a toot. The other driver, a man named Jacomo, who was quite possibly the worst-tempered person Billy had ever met, refused to look over.

It was unfortunate that not all the guides shared Billy's enthusiasm. But what Billy had learned by studying his country's history was that America had been built by opportunists. It was a large and prosperous country and one that could accommodate the less enthused, people like Jacomo, or, for that matter, his pop, who had never showed much enthusiasm for anything aside from Tommy Dorsey and his orchestra. Billy had once caught Pop sitting in his bedroom with the lights out, just after Ma passed, singing "This Is No Dream" to himself in a shy, reedy voice, his socks twitching on the floorboards. Probably Pop had wanted to be a singer; and in another era, one with lots of little villages and people like bards and so forth, he might have been.

But this was America, the land of opportunists, and here it wasn't enough to want something. You had to fight for what you wanted and fight hard, fight through your own resistance and the jeers of others and physical adversity, which was what the Pilgrims had done vis-à-vis the whole Thanksgiving situation, and after them the colonists, who had bucked the most powerful empire on earth even though they were basically just a bunch of underfed tax evaders. And then the pioneers. No, you couldn't forget the pioneers, who had traversed vast prairies and mountains, and battled Indians and grizzly bears and inclement weather and various kinds of pox, and some had even starved and had to eat each other to survive, which, by the way, would make a terrific film treatment, Billy thought, because it said so much about the indomitable spirit that had built the country. Not that cannibalism was part of the indomitable American spirit, but it showed how far some people would go to find good property.

It was a pity that so much of the country was now run based on convenience. Or, more than that, it was really *ironical.* But now that Billy had hitched his wagon to the right dream, he felt much more connected to history, much more like a pioneer, though he was just starting out on his long journey west, and might someday starve and even be forced to eat another person, not literally, but metaphorically. He hoped he would never have to eat another person metaphorically. At the same time, he was aware of the possibility.

The next step for Billy Clamm was to land a role in Sammy Duck's Boston Tea Party reenactment. It was quite ingenious how they staged the performance, especially considering that they used a different boat every day and none of the crew seemed to speak English. The Duckies were hustled on board and Horatio Higgenbottom, intrepid revolutionary agitator, appeared on deck in a long buttoned coat and breeches, and delivered a stirring soliloquy, then flung a wooden box labeled TEA overboard, following which the Duckies joined in until dozens of boxes bobbed in the water and cheers issued forth and the boat spluttered off into international waters, where, if they so chose, guests could gamble by a variety of means while a "British lackey," usually the ill-tempered Jacomo, sallied forth in a motorboat to fetch the tea.

Higgenbottom was clearly the plum role, and sorely in need of a stronger presence. The current player, a Panamanian named Esquivel, lisped his lines. Nothing against Panamanians, but it was an insult to the dramatic moment, the way Esquivel made "tyrannous tax" sound like "tyrweenis tax" and the way he kept scratching at his powdered wig when he should have been *in the moment*, projecting the glory of his role in the coming revolution. Whenever Billy asked about securing a role, Augustino shook his head and held a finger to his lips and peeled Billy's pay from a roll of twenties as fat as an onion.

The light turned green and Billy clicked on his mic and yelled, "Quack! Quack! How many of you Duckies have heard of the Boston Massacre? Well then, we've got something to learn, haven't we? Coming up on our right, you'll note the Old Custom House. It was here, in 1704, that British troops opened fire on a mob of angry colonists. A man named Amos Tuck was struck in the mouth by a bullet. Tuck was a street dancer, and the character on whom Mr. Bojangles was later based. Any Ducky questions?"

A voice behind him said: "Why are the cops arresting your pal back there?"

Billy looked in the rearview mirror. Sure enough, a pair of police cars had pulled over another Duckmobile. "Just a routine traffic violation, Duckies!" As Billy said this, though, he spotted Jacomo beside the vehicle, being jerked into handcuffs and held at gunpoint. Probably his temper had gotten the better of him. Either that or he had warrants. He could see Jacomo as a man with warrants. "Nothing to worry about," he assured his audience.

But just then Billy realized there was indeed something to worry about, because Jacomo had been heading in the same direction he was, to the harbor, which meant that there would be no one to play the British lackey unless he . . . unless Billy himself . . .

Oh, life was good! Life was supremely good, if only one allowed life to be so, and didn't complain incessantly and hit inanimate objects, as Pop so often did; if you didn't deny life, most of all, and remained *connected* to your *process*, because life was really just as much a process as acting was, and maybe even more so in certain settings.

Billy saw his chance, and like Lou Gehrig in that wonderful film *Pride of the Yankees*, he was determined to make the most of it. Not that he didn't feel a kind of kinship with Jacomo, cursing now and spitting at the cops. Jacomo, after all, was really more like poor Wally Pipp. But then Lou Gehrig hadn't had the easiest time of it, either, and had gotten that terrible, vague disease that was in fact so vague they had named it after him.

The scene at the little alcove near the harbor was confusing. A new boat was there, the gangplank down, but Augustino was nowhere to be seen and Esquivel, never a tranquil sort, seemed especially agitated, shouting "Ándele!" and "Vámonos!" and some of the more colorful Panamanian expressions Billy had recently become acquainted with.

"Quack! Quack!" Billy exclaimed. "Time to get your feathers wet, Duckies!"

He hurried toward the little dock where the motorboat was moored and thought about how this was his first big break and how years from now some interviewer, perhaps Diane Sawyer herself, if she were not dead, would look at him meaningfully and say, "What about your first big break, William? Tell *America* about that." And he would think back to this very moment and grin modestly and say, "Diane, I remember as if it were yesterday . . ." Then he lowered himself into the little white boat and waited for the action to begin.

The Duckies shambled up the gangplank, grumbling, which was not unusual, because it was one of those Boston summer days that made you feel as if you were walking around inside a giant mouth. They were met by Esquivel's minions—men in tank tops and shorts, outfits that totally ruined the mood, frankly, the spell—who herded the Duckies onto the bow, or maybe it was the stern. Oddly, none of the other Duckmobiles had appeared. Esquivel checked his watch and frowned. The Duckies sweat quietly under their plastic three-cornered hats. After a tense consultation with his chief minion, Esquivel launched into his speech.

Billy Clamm sat in his motorboat, murmuring along and putting the emphasis on the right words, the words with *dramatic valence*, and feeling certain that if he were the one on deck, with the clip-on microphone and the long buttoned coat, he would be using his arms more, because this was a historic moment after all, the individual throwing off the shackles of anonymity and catapulting himself into history, and for the actor to properly convey this required *broadness of gesture*.

Higgenbottom finished his speech and his minions roused the Duckies and thrust tea boxes into their hands and led them, or in some cases shoved them really, to the railing, and down tumbled the tea into the water. Higgenbottom fired a musket into the air and the ship's engine snorted. This was Billy's cue. He hurried the motorboat out into the bay, waving his own musket about and crying, "Higgenbottom, you bloody scoundrel! This shan't stand!"

That is when the police cars first appeared, tires yelping and sirens and popping lights, though Billy didn't notice them, occupied as he was in demonstrating his British indignity and simultaneously snagging the tea boxes with a small butterfly net. He ignored the commotion around him and focused entirely on finding his inner British lackey. "I'll see your hide tanned upon the royal gallows!" he bellowed. "Knaves, I say! Do you hear me? Dastardly knaves!" Billy wasn't sure what a knave was—it sounded like a fancy flavor of jam—but he was busy brandishing his musket.

Up above, Higgenbottom and his men were scampering about, as if on fire; the Duckies had clamped themselves to the deck. A rippling much like gunfire sounded from the shore. And then, equally distinct, bits of the larger boat began to rain down on him. Billy turned toward shore and saw the police cars. A thicket of rifle barrels poked from above their flung-open doors, and he tried to recall whether any of the previous versions of the Tea Party reenactment had featured this daring postmodern element. Then a strange whizzing kicked up and the net Billy held in his left hand burst into shards. It was at this point he realized something might be awry.

Probably there had been some confusion involving Jacomo. That was Billy's hunch. In any event, once things settled a bit, he would zip back to shore and explain the mix-up, which was, once you got past the use of live ammunition, quite humorous. But then Higgenbottom let out a shriek and hurtled overboard in a cloud of . . . was that actual blood? Billy watched him in awe, admiring the incredibly realistic posture of his falling body and the red swirl created by his flailing limbs, before coming to the reluctant conclusion, as Esquivel smacked the water and torpedoed down, that he was not going *off script* so much as drowning.

Billy's reaction was immediate: he dove beneath the gunwales. A voice, amplified via bullhorn, urged the suspects to "halt at once," urged the suspects to "remain facedown on the deck," urged the suspects, in Spanish, to do something festive-sounding. Then the gunfire started up again and Billy knew that he was best to remain still and wait for law enforcement to get it all straightened out.

He could feel the red stain aflame on his cheek, and with it, the voice of his mother suddenly returned to him. "That's just your way of telling the world you're *alive*." She had said this to soothe him, of course. But the words now seemed to have a different intention altogether. They were her way of recognizing the depth of his passion—a call to arms, or at least to action. Billy watched his hand, in something like amazement, as it grabbed the steering wheel and angled the boat away from the shore. Then his foot slammed the gas pedal.

He was pleased at how well the motorboat handled, especially because he was entering the bay proper at the busiest of times, close to five, when the trawlers from New Bedford made their way in and the frigates and cargo ships lined up for freight. He wended his way among them, watching the dockworkers haul things and spit merrily, and he thought again about Brando and the need to get *inside* the character, and how the great ones never appeared to be acting, only moving through an exquisitely rendered second life.

After an hour trying to locate a place to dock, Billy was hungry. Dusk was coming on, and soon Pop would be wondering where he was and cursing and gazing moonily at the TV. The smell of french fries from the Mickey D's along Mystic would come wafting in the space left by the window unit that had fallen out two summers ago and allegedly struck Miss Jaworski.

But there was nothing to eat in the boat, and no place to dock. Billy focused instead on the dusk, which was quite a thing to see, long shadows and strips of cloud ripening toward purple and the ocean itself reflecting this, turning a color his ma would have called aubergine. Billy had always liked the sound of that word, its connotations, and he realized, with a start, that he had just discovered his stage name.

He turned south, away from the bustle of the bay, down toward the Cape, and when he couldn't see or hear any other boats he shut off the engine and sniffed the salty air and rooted around again to see if Jacomo might have left some emergency rations. The only thing around was a faded life jacket and the boxes of tea. Billy pried one open and inside was a little white vacuum-packed brick. His first thought was that it might be flour and that, if he were a pioneer, he could combine this flour with salt-water so as to produce a sort of primitive bread batter, which, using the heat of the engine, he could bake. But that seemed perhaps far-fetched, given that he had only an outboard motor, and besides, it was probably just baby powder, and so he slit the edge and poked in his pinkie and took a taste. He nearly gagged. Then his gums started to tingle.

So now William Aubergine (né Clamm) was drifting off the coast of Boston at dusk in possession of approximately seven pounds of cocaine. The boat's fuel gauge read close to full, and there was still an hour or more of light. It was all a little daunting to consider.

Old Billy Clamm, predictably enough, was telling himself to turn around and head back *immediately* and try to get all this sorted out. But to William Aubergine, such a course felt like exactly the wrong one, a retreat from the dramatic moment and its possibilities.

He was being given a chance here, the entrée into a new sort of life, and he wasn't just considering the possible proceeds to be had from several pounds of cocaine, though that was not to be overlooked. No, he was considering the new direction his life had taken since he'd decided to act. With the sun dipping toward the water, he did a quick inventory of the coincidences, the *remarkable* coincidences, that had lined up in his favor and brought him to this point, and the responsibility, really, that he faced in living up to such good fortune.

That was the special thing about this country, that you could dream, and that they couldn't take those dreams from you, and the only price was that when the chance came along, the gold ring, or the brass ring, you had to grab at it and not be a scaredy-cat content to live the rest of your life in the sour air of regret. Pop would just have to understand that, and Augustino, and the guys down at Osco. This was America and this was how things sometimes went in America, how the entire enterprise had gotten itself started and grown and prospered. William Aubergine turned the ignition key and listened to the engine rumble, then purr, and he pledged not to forget where he had come from, or the people who lived there, pledged, in other words, to remain *connected* to them no matter what happened next, and he whispered a little prayer of thanks to his ma above as his boat cut a white thread through the water, and imagined himself at the end of a long and arduous day of filming, riding off, as it were, into an actual sunset, or gliding, and feeling that the recent odd events of his life and his gratitude for them would probably seem hokey up there on-screen, especially given the lighting, but that the right actor, rising to the role as required, breathing into it the necessary sense of wonder and hope, would be able to bring the moment off.

DONKEY GREEDY,
DONKEY GETS PUNCHED

DR. RAYMOND OSS had become, in the restless leisure of his late middle age, a poker player. He had a weakness for the game and the ruthless depressives it attracted, one of which he probably was, fair enough, though it wasn't something he wanted known. Oss was a psychoanalyst in private practice and the head of two committees at the San Francisco Institute. He was a short man with a meticulous Trotsky beard and a flair for hats that did not suit him. He cured souls, very expensively, from an office near his home in Los Altos.

On Saturday mornings Oss put on a sweat suit and orthotic tennis shoes and told Sharon he was off to his tai chi class. Then he shot up 101 straight to Artichoke Joe's, in San Bruno, where he played Texas hold 'em at the $3/6 table for five hours straight.

He mucked 80 percent of his hands, bluffed only on the button, and lost a little more than he won.

He didn't mind losing, either, if the cards were to blame. It was only when he screwed up—when he failed to see a flush developing or got slow-played by some grinning Chinese maniac—that he felt the pinch of genuine rage. And even these hands offered a certain masochistic pleasure, a mortification that was swift and public.

It was an inconvenient arrangement, tawdry from certain angles, but Oss couldn't help himself. The moment he spotted the dismal pink stucco of the casino's facade, the sea of bent cigarettes rising from the giant ashtray under the awning, he felt a squirt of brainless adrenaline. He had become addicted to the garlic and ginger prawns, too, a dish so richly infiltrated with MSG that it made his tongue go numb. Sometimes, toward the end of a session, having made his third and final promise to cash in after the next hand, Oss would sit back and let the sensations wash over him: the clack of *pai gow* tiles being stirred, the nimble flicking of the cards, the confusion of colognes and nicotine, the monstrous lonely twitch of the place. He loved Artichoke Joe's, especially while hating it.

ONE DAY, Oss arrived home to find Sharon waiting in his den. She put on a green eyeshade and pulled out a deck of cards and began dealing them onto his Oriental rug. She'd done theater in college.

"How long have you known?"

Sharon frowned.

Jacob (age eleven) had tipped her off, the little shit. "He hacked into your computer," Sharon said.

"I didn't hack into anything," Jacob yelled from the hallway. "I just clicked the History tab for like one second."

Sharon began speaking in her calm social-worker tone. Oss glanced at the scattered cards—a cluster of four hearts, queen high—and thought of his henpecked father. "You could have told me," Sharon said. "I would have understood."

He didn't want his wife's understanding. He had enough of that already. He wanted her indignation, her censure, the stain of his moral insufficiencies tossed between them like a bet. But she saw his Duplicity and raised her Forgiveness.

So he bid Artichoke Joe's farewell—farewell, green felt! farewell, ginger prawns!—and started playing in a weekly game with fellow analysts. The twenty-dollar buy-in, the nonalcoholic beer, the arthritic dithering over a seventy-five-cent raise: it was his penance.

Overall, he felt himself vaguely improved. He began to hike the Stanford hills and reread Dostoyevsky and brought Sharon to the Swiss Alps for a month. His older son, Ike, insisted on calling him "Cisco," it being his impression that the Cisco Kid had been a famous gambler. Jacob continued to sneak into his office in the hopes of catching him playing online. "Check it before you wreck it, daddio," he warned. Oss wanted very much to strike the boy, just once, near the eye.

GARY SHARPE APPEARED in his office that fall. Oss would recall this coincidence later with an odd blend of pride and shame. Sharpe was tall, pale, handsome in a sneering way. He sat miserably and squinted. "So how's this work? Do I hand you my checkbook now, or wait till the end of the session?"

"This is a consultation," Oss said. "We're merely trying—"

"Or maybe I should just dump the cash at your feet?"

Oss sighed without appearing to. It was one of his tricks. "Small, unmarked bills work best. Now why don't you tell me why you're here."

Sharpe shook his head. "My wife."

"She suggested you come?"

"Suggested. You could say that. She's a shrink, too. Her supervisor is some pal of yours. Dr. Penn. I'm not sure how it works with you people. She feels I'm depressed owing to unresolved issues with my father, who, by the way, died when I was seventeen. So technically I have issues with my dead father."

"And you feel?"

Sharpe inspected his fingernails. "I'm in a volatile business. I've explained this to her a few thousand times."

"You're not depressed, then?"

"Depressed. Christ. Whatever happened to *sad*? I guess there's no dough in sadness. As for your next question, yeah, I've done the drugs. Paxil, Wellbutrin, some new one they've got called Kweezlemonkey. That one goes up your ass as a minty fresh gel."

Oss laughed. "Sounds refreshing."

"Right. I get the funny shrink. Perfect." Sharpe fake-yawned. He looked as if he hadn't slept in a few weeks.

"Are you aware of what an analysis entails?"

"My wife filled me in. I lie on my back and complain about what an asshole everyone is. Then, when you've made enough to pay for your new deck, the angels blow a trumpet and I'm cured. What a fucking racket. You people should carry guns."

"I do," Oss said.

Sharpe would be back, the bluster said as much. He'd blame it on his wife for a few weeks, then they could begin the work. "What is it exactly you do, Mr. Sharpe?"

"I play cards," he said. "I take money from people who don't want it anymore."

SO THIS WAS HIS NEW PATIENT: Gary "Card" Sharpe, winner of the 2003 World Series of Poker, enfant terrible of the World Poker Tour, notorious for his table talk, his braying laugh, his signature line of poker-themed clothing and paraphernalia (Look Sharpe™).

On Friday, Oss saw Penn in the parking garage.

"Thanks for the referral."

Penn, who smiled incessantly, smiled. "One greedy prick deserves another." He zapped his trunk open and began removing stuffed animals. Penn was always doing things like this, things that made no sense. "His wife's a real sweetheart. She'll leave him if he doesn't shape up."

"No pressure, though."

"Take it as a compliment. You'll know what he's talking about, anyway. All the lingo. Down and dirty. Double down."

Oss took off his derby and inspected the rim. "I wasn't aware you considered me such an expert at poker."

"I wasn't aware you considered me such an idiot." Penn tapped his brow with a yellow monkey. "Come on, Ray. Tai chi? How long have I known you?"

"He's going to hassle me about the fee nonstop."

"Of course he is," Penn replied. "He's a gambler. That's how he keeps score. Speaking of which, you in Friday?"

Penn played in the weekly game. He held his cards as if the ink were still wet and studied them like runes. Then he lost cheerfully. Everyone loved Penn, in the same way they sort of hated Oss.

SHARPE RESENTED THE PHYSICAL ARRANGEMENT of analysis, that he had to lie down with Oss seated behind him. He spent the early weeks of treatment insulting the decor: the blond wooden end tables and antique rugs. "What do you call this look? *Freud gets gangbanged by Ikea*?"

For the most part, Sharpe talked poker. His disquisitions inevitably began, "You know what I fucking hate?" He fucking hated the Internet. He fucking hated the TV coverage. He fucking hated the travel.

"You ever been in the Reno airport before dawn, Oss?"

"Can't say I've had the pleasure."

"It's like hell with slot machines. Even the air smells sad. Care to guess why I was there so early? So I could get back from a tournament in time for this shit-ass session."

"How'd you do?"

Sharpe blew a raspberry. "Twelve K, plus sponsor money. We wound up chopping the pot at the final table. You know what that means? It means we got rid of all the donkeys, the shit players, then split the prize money."

"Sounds like easy money," Oss said.

Sharpe bristled. "Easy?" he said.

"I just meant—"

"I know what you meant," Sharpe said. "I'm sure a guy in your position—you don't think playing poker takes much brainpower, do you? It's just a bunch of cigar smoke and dumb luck. What's your game anyway, Doc? Bridge? You probably sit around on Saturday night playing penny-a-point, creaming your fucking chinos because somebody made small slam in spades." Sharpe's upper lip curled. "You know who you fucking remind me of? My fucking dad."

Now we're getting somewhere, Oss thought. He waited a moment before asking, "How so?"

"Oh, you'd like that, wouldn't you?"

Oss sighed his silent sigh. "This isn't a poker game, Gary. You don't win by hiding your cards."

"I don't win at all," Sharpe said. "I just give all the chips to you."

"I can only help if you're forthcoming with me."

Sharpe exhaled through his nose. "So now you're Dr. Phil? Dr. Phil: the midget version with the stupid hats." He sneered. "What the fuck is up with these hats, anyways? You're bald, Doc. Deal with it."

OSS WAS SECRETLY THRILLED to be treating Sharpe. The depth of his rage was refreshing. It returned Oss to his adolescence, to the loathing he had so lavishly apportioned to his own father, who sold hardware, who developed pathetic infatuations with his prominent customers. (My good friend Dr. Lindell. My good friend Magistrate Johns.) The old man, with his Brooklyn brogue and small-time dreams. "A man who gambles," he liked to say, "is a man who doesn't want his shoit."

Sharpe could be tender, too. He was terrified of losing his wife. "Back in college, she figured I'd go to some hedge fund. I told her as much. Look: she's not thrilled with the choices I've made. But she's got a better heart than me. That's more or less the basis of our marriage."

Oss was stunned to discover that Sharpe had a child as well, a boy named Doyle. "Sharp little bastard," Sharpe said. "He slaughters me at everything. Concentration. Go Fish."

"A born card counter, eh?"

"No no no," Sharpe said. "He's not going to wind up rotting in some casino. He's got a real imagination."

"Poker doesn't require imagination?"

"Donkey greedy. Donkey gets punched. The rest is just math. He gets the creative stuff from Kate, these crazy little comic books he draws, he does all the plots himself. Seven years old! Every dad says this shit, I guess. But, you know, sometimes he looks at me and I'll realize for a second how fragile he is. It makes me want to cry." Sharpe swallowed hard; his ear flushed for a moment. "I have no idea why. It's like I want to protect him from some terrible thing and I don't even know what."

OSS URGED SHARPE TO THINK about what that thing might be, but by the next session, he'd retreated to the old troughs of grievance. "You know what I fucking hate," he said. "All these guys from Google, with their mirror shades and their goatees. Chin pussies, I call them. You can't swing a dead cat in Artichoke Joe's without hitting Google trash."

Oss froze for a moment.

"What?" Sharpe said. "Why'd you stop taking notes?"

Oss sat back and scratched out *Did-not-Did-not-Did-not.* "You were saying?" he said.

"Wait a second." Sharpe smiled. "I just said something that threw you off. Don't bullshit a bullshitter, Doc."

Oss's tongue tingled. He could taste the ginger prawns. "I suppose I was surprised you'd play at a local casino. Wouldn't people recognize you?"

"Of course they fucking recognize me."

"But wouldn't that make it tough? Why would anyone play against you?"

Sharpe did his full-throated bray. "You're kidding, right? Everyone in that place wants to play me. For fuck's sake. I'm like Barry Bonds to these donks. Only they can play against me. They can even beat me. Shit. It's mostly up to the cards."

"I see," Oss said. For a moment he imagined what it might be like to sit across the table from Sharpe, the sort of irrational hatred a guy like him could generate.

"That's what I hate about these Google dweebs. They've got all this dumb money, more than they can spend. So they throw it at me for a few hours and brag about that one gutshot they hit for the next ten years. That's not gambling, it's Disneyland. Gambling is about people ruining their fucking lives."

"So that's your goal? To ruin your life?"

Sharpe's brow crimped and Oss, studying his face from behind, noticed for the first time that the sneer on his lip was in fact the result of a small scar.

"You have to realize what you are," Sharpe said. "If you're a gambler, you're a gambler. That's how your nerves fire. I wake up every morning thinking about that next great hand. You can get all high-and-mighty and call that an addiction. Or you can call it what it is: a fucking desire. I'll tell you this, there's nothing sadder than a gambler in denial. I should know. My dad was one."

Oss waited for Sharpe to elaborate. It was a lot of what he did. The silence dragged on.

"What?" Sharpe said finally. "What the fuck do you want from me?"

IN JULY, Sharpe returned from the World Series of Poker in a black mood. He'd been knocked out of the tournament on the third day, a humiliation Oss had witnessed (with some relish) on ESPN2.

"I've got a tell," Sharpe said to Oss now. "I fucking know it. There's no other way . . . You know what a tell is, right? That's like something that gives away how you feel. Like that swallowed-sigh thing you do when you're frustrated. That's a tell."

Oss sat back in his chair.

"This is what I do for a living, okay, Doc? I read people. We're in the same business that way, only I look them in the eye before I take their money. Now I need some fucking help from you for once, because obviously I'm doing something I'm not aware of."

"What happened?"

Sharpe threw up his hands as if he were tossing a salad, a salad at which he was furious. "Bad cards. Bad beats. That I can handle. I'll scrape by with shit luck. But this was different. I let it get personal, which is rule one: it's never personal. Because how else does Bill Tandy sniff out three bluffs in a row?"

"Who's Bill Tandy?"

"My exact fucking point." Sharpe closed his eyes. "This guy, Mr. Retired Real Estate Puke from Tucson, he sits there eyeballing me for ten seconds and suddenly he pops his tongue under his lip, which is what he does when he knows he's got a guy beat—it's *his* tell."

From where he was sitting, Oss could see the cuff of Sharpe's right ear redden again. "Couldn't he have just been guessing?" Oss said.

"He had jack-high crap," Sharpe muttered. "You don't guess against me with jack-high crap. Even an old donkey knows that.

No, he saw something. This fucker saw something. And I want you to tell me what."

"Me?"

"I've been paying you a grand a week. You're supposed to be so observant, so wise to my subconscious. It's about time you offered some return on my investment."

"I didn't realize it was my job to make you a better poker player," Oss said.

Sharpe glared at the ceiling. "It's your job to make me a happier person, you little shit."

"Winning doesn't seem to make you a happier person, Gary."

"Meaning what?"

Oss remained silent.

"You are a complete french-fried asshole, Oss. I pity your fucking wife and the disfigured dwarf children that sprang from her loins. Honestly. You're worse than my old man."

"I take it he didn't approve of your career."

Sharpe snorted. "No, he didn't. And he spanked me on my little bum in front of all my friends and I cried and cried. Wah-wah-wah. Then I tried to kill him, but I went blind instead and stumbled into a giant cave that smelled like my mother's snatch. God, you're obvious."

As a younger analyst, Oss would have laughed and let Sharpe jump the hook. But he had come to recognize disgust as the first form of disclosure. "You said earlier that your father was a gambler in denial. What did you mean?"

Sharpe let out an exasperated sigh. "He worked in the financial sector. He played the market. That's all I meant. All those guys are gamblers. The whole fucking thing's a big bet."

"What happened to him?"

"He made a bad bet."

"And?"

"And he hung himself."

Was this another bluff? It was hard to tell with Sharpe.

When he finally spoke again his voice had lost its belligerence. It wasn't soft so much as deflated. "My dad made his nut off something called portfolio insurance. The idea was that you paid a premium to limit your losses. Then came the crash of '87 and the whole thing blew up." Sharpe shook his head. "And the reason it blew up is simple: he was selling the fantasy of risk-free gambling—which doesn't exist. So he lost everything and took some rope out to the garage and my mom and me were left to scrounge through his estate for rent money." Sharpe smiled his sneering smile. "This is the guy who lectured me about responsibility, about doing the right thing."

Oss didn't say anything for a time. He thought, oddly, of his own father, the way he fingered each coin from his palm onto the counter when making a purchase. Pop was a child of the Depression. He had tasted poverty. And still, Oss found his elaborate caution around money shameful.

"I can see why you might be angry at him," Oss said.

Sharpe closed his eyes. "I'm not angry," he said. The cuff of his ear flushed. "He had a shitty hand and he lost. The end."

IT WASN'T AS IF the discoloration was obvious. You'd really have to be looking to notice it. But then, that was what pros did. They looked for signs.

Oss's first impulse was to drop a hint, maybe suggest a longer hairstyle. But the more he pondered the matter, the more misguided this seemed. His role was to help the patient come to terms with the unbearable facts and feelings of his history. In fact, it was the loss at poker that had induced Sharpe (finally) to discuss his father. Was it also true that Oss derived a certain pleasure from withholding? That it served as a form of revenge against an equally withholding and, at times, emotionally abusive patient? Possibly.

One thing was clear: the closer Sharpe drew to the sources of his depression, the more recalcitrant he became. One swelter-ing August afternoon, he showed up in an obvious state of in-ebriation. "I've had a few," was how he put it.

"Any particular reason?" Oss said.

"A few works better than one." Sharpe belched. "Anyways, I've decided you want me to lose. The sadder and more fucked up I become, the more dough you make."

"You're my bread and butter?"

"You said it, Ossipoo." Sharpe shuffled an invisible stack of chips.

"You also get off on looking down on me. You think I'm some cretin. Like I should read more books or something."

Oss thought of Dostoyevsky's gambler, Alexei. He had always imagined the character in a green velvet waistcoat, watching the roulette wheel spin. Freud argued that Dostoyevsky—like most gamblers—subconsciously wanted to lose. He sought to punish himself for the death of his parents. His father had been a vi-cious drunk, murdered by his serfs, supposedly. The novelist had done that one better, letting Smerdyakov, the bastard son, do the deed. Was there no love so disastrous as that between a son and father? Oss himself was still a wreck when it came to his pop, whose gentle hand he had held even as death took him under.

"Are you fucking listening to me?" Sharpe said.

"Of course," Oss said.

"What was I just talking about?"

Oss stared down at his notes. Absurdly, his eyes were stinging.

"You were asking me, for perhaps the hundredth time, why you should keep coming here."

"And?"

"We are trying to understand your discontent. This is not easy work," Oss said.

"Oh, for fuck's sake."

◆   ◆   ◆

SHARPE BEGAN TRAVELING OVERSEAS on what he called "the sheik circuit." Dubai, Abu Dhabi. "Hey," he said, when Oss complained about missed sessions, "the price is right. You want I should ask any of them if they need a nice Jewy analyst?" He continued to appear for sessions drunk. He flew into paranoid rages. He celebrated his year anniversary as a patient by presenting Oss with a bill for forty-eight thousand dollars, requesting a full refund for "failure to deliver the contracted services."

Oss prescribed medications intended to ameliorate the bipolar symptoms. He urged Sharpe to cut back on alcohol and poker. Sharpe responded by flouting his bills.

A week before Thanksgiving, he shambled in and nodded at Oss's hat rack. "Tell me you didn't wear the fucking beret outside this office. Christ. You're like a one-man stupid-looking contest." He plopped down on his back. His unlaced sneakers thwacked the couch.

"We've discussed payment at length. That discussion is now over. You either pay your outstanding fees or we terminate."

"Would you accept chips?" Sharpe reached into his pocket. "No? Ooooh, the silent treatment. I must be in trouble."

"You're not a child, Gary."

"I love it when you get all stern, Doc. I really do. It makes me think of me dear old dad!" Sharpe rubbed at his eyes dramatically. "He was a lot like you, Ossipoo, a little donkey who thought he was a big shark. And look how that turned out. You know what he was wearing when I found him swinging from the rafters?"

"Hold on a moment," Oss said.

"A silk ascot. Right under the rope. I shit you not. He's got the fat blue face, his tongue's hanging out, his eyes about to pop from their sockets, there's shit dripping from his pants, and the stupid fuck—"

"Is this true?" Oss said. "If this is true—"

But Sharpe had said too much. They both knew it. "You think I need this shit? You think I ever needed this shit?" He laughed, but his voice cracked around the sound. "Fuck you, Doc. No, seriously. We're done here."

It was a sad moment for Oss, because he loved his patients, even the difficult ones, for the weaknesses they laid before him, for their courage, and because it had been Sharpe, after all, who looked like an animal, a beast of burden, charging blindly from the office, off into a world that could bring him no peace.

"YOU DID WHAT YOU HAD TO DO," said Penn, to whom Oss inevitably and resentfully confided. "Some patients can't be saved."

Sharon was less sympathetic. "He sounds like a royal asshole," she said that evening.

"Mom said 'a-hole'!" Jacob shrieked.

"Shut up," Oss snapped. "Shut your mouth until further notice."

Jacob held his cheek as if he'd been slapped. Sharon stared at Oss in horror.

"The kid has to learn not to be a tattletale," Oss said. "All right, look. I apologize. It's been a long day."

Oss tried to put Gary Sharpe out of mind. But he kept turning up: on the poker shows, loud and unhappy, with bloodshot eyes. Oss missed him. While his other patients murmured their soft complaints, his mind drifted to desirable poker hands. Ace/jack suited. Pocket queens. He found himself volunteering to do weekend Costco runs, knowing these would lead him past Artichoke Joe's. He limited himself to one game per month, then two.

It was nearly a year later, on a sleepy Tuesday afternoon, that Oss looked up from his seat and saw his former patient striding across the casino floor. He wore a tracksuit the same color as his stubble. Oss knew he should muck his hand and slip out quietly. But he hesitated just long enough to allow Sharpe to spot him.

There was a buzz in the place by now, several folks at his elbow. Sharpe made straight for Oss. "Don't I know you?" he said.

Oss looked up and smiled.

"How the hell are you?" Sharpe seemed genuinely glad to see him. "I didn't realize you played here."

"I don't, really. Occasionally."

The other players at the table stared at Oss in astonishment. *You're pals with Gary Sharpe*, their eyes said. *Really?*

The manager of the poker section hurried over to genuflect. Sharpe stepped away from the table so they could finish up the hand. He did some backslapping, signed one of his hats for a trembling Indian kid, posed for photos. Then he smiled and nodded at an empty seat across from Oss. "Mind if I join you gents?"

"We're happy to start a no-limit table," the manager said.

"No no," Sharpe said. "Just want to play a few hands. No big deal."

"You can have my seat," Oss said. "I was just about to cash out."

"Come on now," Sharpe said. "You're going to hurt my feelings, Doc." He dropped into the empty seat. "I was hoping you might teach me a few things."

The dealer glanced at Oss. Staying at the table was clearly the wrong thing to do on about six levels. But the air around him was crackling with a strange electricity. The biddings of fate. He nodded and let the cards come.

It was immediately obvious the speed with which Sharpe processed information: table position, pot odds. His eyes flicked from face to face on the flop. It was something like watching a shark—the grace and efficiency of his aggression. His outbursts, so petulant on TV, came off as charming in person, a way of relieving the essential tedium of the game.

When Oss took a pot with two small pairs, Sharpe applauded. "Thattaboy," he said.

For his part, Oss avoided looking at Sharpe, in particular his ears.

"How you two know each other?" the dealer said.

"Doc was an adviser of mine for a time." Sharpe grinned. "He has, despite that idiotic Greek fisherman's cap, a keen financial sense."

Everyone laughed.

"What kind of advice you give?" the dealer said.

"The expensive kind," Sharpe roared.

Oss waited for the laughter to subside. "How are things going?" he asked.

"My wife's going to take 50 percent of everything." Sharpe downed the rest of his beer and gestured for another. "Luckily everything's offshore, so there's that."

"I'm so sorry," Oss said.

Sharpe sneered. "It's not like I'm going to kill myself."

Oss wanted to pull him aside, to talk to him privately. But they were at the poker table, a place where the only intimacy permitted was between a man and his own fortune. It was time for Oss to go. The problem—and it really was a problem—was that he'd been dealt two cards by now. Good cards.

These were in fact the best cards he'd gotten all day. The bet came to him and he raised. Everyone folded except Sharpe, who was the big blind. "Alone at last," he said.

Oss laughed uncomfortably.

The flop came:

This gave Oss two pair, aces and kings, an exceptional hand. He thought briefly about checking. Perhaps it was best to get through the hand and get out. Instead he bet the limit.

Sharpe glanced at Oss. "Mighty proud of that pair, are you? I'd be, too. But you shouldn't tell the whole table, Doc." He inhaled loudly through his nose. Oss realized, with a start, that Sharpe was imitating him.

"That's cold," someone murmured.

"No, that's poker," Sharpe snapped. "I just did the good doctor a big favor. Saved him a bundle down the line. More than he ever did for me." He took a slug of his new beer. "I raise."

Oss could feel the room start to thrum. He looked at the flop again and did some quick math. The chances that Sharpe had three of a kind were one in twenty-five hundred. He might be playing for the club flush, but that was a dumb bet. "Reraise," Oss said.

Sharpe smiled. "Oh for fuck's sake, Doc. You already cost me fifty grand. What's a little more?"

The turn card was the two of clubs.

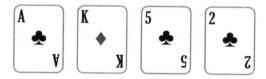

If Sharpe was looking for a flush, he'd just made it. He might also have a three/four, which would give him a straight, though that would mean he'd drawn to an inside straight, something he would never do. No, if anything, Sharpe had the flush. But the odds on that were one in five. Two pair still made Oss a heavy favorite.

"I'll bet," he said. "I don't think you have the flush."

"You're right," Sharpe said unhappily. "But I'll raise anyway."

Oss looked up. A small crowd had begun to form. Or maybe

it had been there all along, to watch the great Gary Sharpe clobber some poor donkey. That's what he was to these folks: a donkey. A dilettante with a nasty little midweek habit. They were just waiting for him to fold.

"Reraise."

Sharpe sat back. Another beer had disappeared down his throat. "Well now, Doc, I hope those oats feel good. But do me a favor, since you're so confident: let's at least stop playing kiddie poker."

He turned to the manager. "Can we make this a no-limit game?"

The crowd let out a murmur.

The manager said, "It's a limit table, Gary. I really can't do that."

"A little side wager, then? How about that?"

The manager regarded Sharpe with bureaucratic despair. "The casino cannot be party to any such arrangement. That'd be between you gentlemen."

"Excellent," Sharpe said. "I'd say we've got enough witnesses. So what if we say I see your six, and raise you ten thousand dollars on the side."

Oss cleared his throat. "You're kidding, I assume."

"No, sir."

"I think it's best if we just stick to the table limits."

Sharpe began nodding. "Oh, I see. You just want to play the safe game, nothing that could get you hurt. Does your wife even know you're here, Doc? How fucking sad."

Oss glanced at Sharpe's ears, just for a second. He knew it was some kind of violation—of analytic trust, of basic decency—but he couldn't restrain himself. They were as pale as the rest of him.

"What's the matter, Doc? You don't look so hot." Sharpe called out for another beer. "All right. Listen. I'm gonna do you another favor, for old times' sake. In front of all these nice folks and God himself, I'm gonna tell you to fold. Just throw your cards in the middle of the table and be done with it, son. Go home and tell your wife a good lie."

It was an astonishing display. A few people in the crowd whistled. Someone said, "Classic Sharpe."

Oss reached for his cards. He certainly meant to fold, to put an end to this folly. But he paused for a moment first.

Sharpe gulped at his beer. "Okay, we're all done here, folks. The good doctor is all done pretending. That's okay, Doc. Just walk away. There's no shame when you're beat." The cuff of his right ear flushed. "You want to see the hand you lost to? Would that help?" Sharpe made as if to reach for his cards. His ear had gone crimson now.

Oss felt his chest start to fizz. His hands, which had been hovering over his cards, trembled. He clasped them together and nearly burst into laughter. "I appreciate all your kind advice," he said. "But I guess I'll have to call anyway."

The crowd let out a whoop.

"Okay," Sharpe said loudly. "I tried. I honestly tried. I'm no longer responsible for what happens next. That's on you, Doc."

Oss realized, with a twinge of pity, that Sharpe was trapped. He'd gotten himself in too deep, allowed it to become personal.

The dealer turned over the river card. It was the ace of spades. The board now looked like this:

Oss couldn't quite believe his eyes. He'd hit a full house on the river, aces over kings. Even if Sharpe wasn't bluffing, even if he'd made his flush, Oss had him beat. It seemed almost cruel.

Sharpe glanced at the fifth card, as if it was of no great

concern to him. "One more round of betting," he said. "You feeling lucky?"

"Check," Oss said.

"Ten thousand," Sharpe said. He was plainly out of his mind.

Oss cleared his throat again. "Listen," he said, "I think this has gone far enough."

Sharpe turned to the crowd and brayed. "I'm not sure if you're entirely familiar with your options here, Doc. You've got three: call, raise, or fold."

"Okay," Oss said. "I get it."

But Sharpe wasn't done. He was never done. "More than a year of my life you wasted with your overpriced psychobabble bullshit," he murmured. "And here's the funny part: you actually think that shit matters, that you're saving people with your little spells and incantations. Are you starting to get it? This is what matters, right here." He gestured to the cards that lay between them, then to the crowd. "So don't disappoint all these nice folks, Doc. They came here to see what happens next."

Oss closed his eyes and considered how he had arrived at this point. He knew some of it was his fault. But was it his fault that he'd been dealt such a hand? Was it his fault that his opponent was a psychotic asshole? Hell, if anything, he'd tried to help the psychotic asshole.

Sharpe was now leering at him (psychotically) and blowing beer fumes across the table. "Be a good boy," he bellowed. "Save your shirt. Remember: guys like me always beat guys like you."

"Double it," Oss said.

He couldn't quite believe the words had come out of his mouth. He honestly hadn't meant to say them. But the moment he did, his body surged with joy. He felt as if he might be floating. "Double it," he said again.

The crowd erupted in murderous approval. The manager drew a cell phone from his pocket and dialed frantically.

"Let's make it an even forty," Sharpe shot back. He was slurring now. "That's right. Forty thousand, you greedy bastard. You want to hang yourself in public, here's your chance. I can't save you."

A great calm descended on Oss. He had seen patients for more than half his life. Whatever tumult they created in the present, it all traced back to the past. Whatever wrath they aimed at him, he was merely a hired stand-in. And so here was the famous Gary Sharpe, face-to-face at last with his father. He wanted to destroy the old man, but deep down he wanted to destroy himself more.

He'd been unable to convince Sharpe on the analytic couch. But perhaps here, at the poker table, which had become his refuge, his final hiding place, the lesson might stick. "Let's make it an even fifty thousand dollars," Oss said.

"Okay now," said the manager, "now that, that's the final raise, okay? Okay, guys? I don't care what the private arrangement is."

The crowd hissed, but Sharpe held up his hands for silence. He looked remarkably serene, resigned to his fate. "Fair enough," he said. "I call. Now do what you came here to do, Doc. No hard feelings." He leered again and Oss saw not the garish smile but the faint scar on his lip. It made him want to weep, to see how far human beings would go to hide from the truth of themselves.

There was nothing else for him to do, though, so Oss turned over his cards. He could hear the crowd roar. "I'm sorry," he said. "I truly am. I didn't want it to come to this."

"Sure you did," Sharpe said. He smiled gently. Then he turned over his cards:

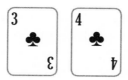

There was a moment of confused silence, then the crowd let out a collective gasp. "Take a good look," Sharpe said.

Oss inspected the community cards again. The green felt took on a queasy shimmer. He saw Sharpe's hand now:

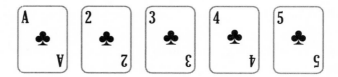

The shock hit Oss in waves. The nerves in his neck constricted. He was having trouble breathing. All around him was noise and jostling. Two or three people reached to comfort him. Sharpe rose from his seat and walked around the table. He squatted down and gestured for the others to step back.

Oss stared at his ears, which were blazing.

"Yeah, my wife was kind enough to tip me off, just before she gave me the boot. And you know the crazy thing? Alcohol has the exact same physiological effect on me. Imagine that! What are the odds?"

Oss found that his hands were still clasped, but there was no feeling in either of them. It was as if he were dead now, as if he were holding the hand of his own dead father.

"Now don't go worrying about the dough. We can set up a payment plan, something weekly." Sharpe tried for a grin, but it wouldn't hold.

"What in God's name have I done?" Oss whispered. He suspected he was weeping. His cheeks certainly felt wet.

"Settle down now, Doc." Oss felt a hand laid upon his shoulder with unbearable tenderness. The room was a bright blur, at the center of which hovered Sharpe's face; the sneer was gone, replaced by a familiar sorrow. Already his triumph was slipping away, into the unbending shadows of vengeance. "The man who can't lose always does," he said softly. "Did you learn nothing from our work?"

HOPE WOOD

MR. ALBERT WAS OUT FRONT OF HIS PLACE when Sligo and I arrived, dabbing trim onto an antique cash register. He painted everything in and around his home eventually, using the high-gloss exterior stuff from little cans. He did characters, too: yellow giraffes spotted in red and cows with motors where their udders should have been, and chariots with little black boys carried along by giant brown horses. The work was lousy with redemption. You couldn't look at it for very long without wanting to forgive someone.

Sligo and I were on hand to inventory Mr. Albert's basement, a project that smacked of honest labor and the chance to put things in order. He wanted to know why we were late. Being unemployed philosophers, recent graduates in fact, we were often late. I could see Sligo battling the urge to curse the law officer who had rather mercifully impounded his Tercel.

The warehouse across the street was coming apart in crinkled sheets, tin or something cheaper than tin. The sun pressed down like a thumb. Everything recommended a lemonade stand. But the streets were desolate and striped with tar. Once in a while a cop car crawled past, bound for some forsaken village of women and children.

Mr. Albert lived in a cape bungalow, its window frames painted such that the dwelling appeared to be batting its eyelashes. His official studio was inside, but he did most of his work on the porch, or the lawn. Sligo danced up the steps, cha-cha-cha, and punched a button on the register. The cash drawer popped with a hopeful chime.

Mr. Albert tapped him on the forehead with two fingers. "Somebody tell you to make a fuss?" His voice sounded like a torn reed. Flecks of paint had settled the thin riverbeds around his eyes. His hands were the most beautiful things I'd ever seen. The knuckles looked like gardenia bulbs. "All right, then," he said, licking his teeth.

We followed him into the house, past the dead jukebox, the mirrored chifforobe, the small pink-and-blue bedroom where, presumably, he retired with lady friends on those nights given over to "necessary fleshly libations," as he called them.

The cellar light was busted and Sligo put his foot through one of the steps at the bottom and something went *bang* and a dog came bounding out of the wood-rotten darkness. It looked to be auditioning for wolfdom. Sligo let out a girlish noise.

"There's a dog down here!" I yelled up the stairs.

"I been looking for that dog," Mr. Albert called down.

Sligo flicked his boot at the animal as we waited for our pupils to adjust. The dog gazed at us with dog pity. No challenge here, those eyes said.

"Settle down, Maggie," Sligo said. He called all dogs Maggie, for whatever reason.

Things had turned tense for the two of us. Summer had lowered the boom and nobody could afford air-conditioning. Already our framed degrees were wilting. The future which we had talked about eagerly for years was upon us and our shock was not that this future should entail depression—which, idiotically, we took as a measure of our depth—but that it should prove so *uninteresting*.

There were other factors. Sligo's girlfriend, a white-throated Virginian with plantations of money and erratic hygiene, had announced her impregnation some weeks earlier. Sligo, a Catholic of broad and indefinite beliefs, was convinced now that he wanted the child, his child, though it seemed plain to the rest of us that he wanted a drama large enough to impose on his vanity. He'd spent the last few weeks of school rampaging through the theology of the Middle Ages in search of an irrefutable argument for God's existence.

My own girl, Julia Weiss, had turned on me. Overnight, my flesh had become a mortification to her. My flesh *was* pretty much a mortification. It was her great calm about it, so eerily akin to truth, that frightened me.

The basement rolled out in front of us like the damp hold of a vast ark. Bureaus and rocking chairs and ottomans and hope chests stacked one on another, in leggy strata. Cedar, maple, mahogany, beech. Everything on top of everything else, chipped, water-stained, peeling and scrolling in the dankness. A vintage fan stood against the far wall, blades painted in dust.

"Very come-as-you-are," Sligo said. "Very *Guernica*."

Mr. Albert had been stockpiling furniture for years. On garbage days he cruised his Buick through the tony precincts of Winston-Salem, plucking crippled chairs and dressers from the curbs. The drug boys and their jittery clients brought him offerings, which he never refused and sometimes paid for. His vocation as a furniture repairman left him vulnerable to wood. He ran his knotted fingers along the grains with absentminded devotion. Mr. Albert had been many things: sharecropper, private first class, factory worker, chauffeur. Mostly these days he painted—"drawing," he called it—selling to peach-skinned matrons from across town who fluttered over him as if he were some sensationally trained monkey and failed to recognize that they were buying back their own settees and porch swings.

We'd met Mr. Albert inside the Po' Folks on Lee, where Sligo came for the all-you-can-eat pork buffet. Later, during one of his restless walkabouts, Sligo had spotted Mr. Albert's house. The colors had come rushing at him—colors so bright, he told me, he could taste them. Mr. Albert invited him in, and Sligo launched into his case against the Neoplatonists. Mr. Albert, in turn, complained about the dereliction of his staff, his staff being a young cousin named Boo Boo, who was, however implausibly, lazier than Sligo. Our sole drawing card was availability.

Now there was this ongoing inventory process, more of an untangling really, five bucks an hour plus dinner. You couldn't have found a worse couple of day laborers. We were soft from years of heuristic endeavor. We couldn't quite get the knack of moving actual weight against actual gravity. The universe of balance and angles eluded us.

"Can't we chop away some of these steps?" Sligo said.

We were banging around some kind of art deco cupboard.

"Hernia," I said.

"Yeah," he said. "Yeah, hernia."

Mr. Albert stood at the top of the stairs. He looked disappointed in the entire species.

"Maybe if we turn it around."

"The other way?"

"Fuck."

"Keep going."

"Where?"

"*That* end."

"Pinching! Pinching!"

"Down?"

And so on.

We heaved up through the blackness, toward the doorway. Sweat ran down our forearms and stung our blistered hands. Outside, in the miraculous world of air, sunlight fretted the lawn. Mr. Albert called out instructions in his teakettle tremolo. He was painting an antique crib, lining the headboard with flowers and girls.

Sligo's eyes puddled up. "I see myself as a father." He gazed at the crib. "I'm not *frightened* of that."

"Let's just finish the job," I said. "Come on. He's paying by the hour."

"Look at it, Mikey. It's unflawed. It's perfect."

I could smell an outburst in the offing, like seaside rain. "Food only happens when we're done," I reminded him.

Mr. Albert looked up. "Bring that dog up here," he said. "I got to have a talk with that dog."

The fourth piece we did was a rolltop desk with a hidden compartment. I got my head practically stuck inside its drawer.

"Aquinas worked on a desk like this," Sligo announced. We were only a couple of steps from the top, but I felt my foot sliding. Soon, momentarily I mean, the desk would come clobbering down on my face.

"Lift your side," I pleaded.

"Do your fingers hurt?" Sligo said.

I could envision a child dying in his care. Easily. "I'm falling. Jesus. Please." And my foot did give way, and I did stumble. But Sligo managed to cantilever the desk on the top step.

"What's the idea?" he said, grunting.

When we got outside again, Mr. Albert told us to stop, just stop. "Like watching a duck swim ass up."

"We were just getting the hang of it," Sligo said. He sidled over to the crib and touched the unpainted panel. It was a strange grain, spiked in the way of pine but with a loping regularity, like the line on a heart monitor. "What kind of wood is this?"

"Hope wood," Mr. Albert said.

"Hope wood?"

"What my daddy called it. Don't come across it too much anymore. Some kind of old ash, maybe. Smells like licorice."

Sligo bent to sniff the wood, but Mr. Albert shooed him away. "Don't get into all that," he said. "We got to go in the car."

He wanted us both in the back. His years as a chauffeur made him that way. He drove with the touching obliviousness of one who assumes the roadways have not changed in thirty years. We glided past the Hanes complex, where smocked workers bent to help machines assemble undergarments; past the lumberyards, which smelled of sap and gasoline. Farther down, they put together televisions, cigarettes, soda pop, pacifiers. They had factories for all the important addictions.

The streets were speckled with loss in six-foot postures. "Look at all this trash," Mr. Albert said. "I got six children and not one of them in the street. Problem with these boys is they don't *want* the work. They got drugs and pussy and rap music all up in their head."

It was like listening to Pat Buchanan.

"Mr. Joe Kleinberg, that was the man I drove for—now that man was a genius. He was practically the secretary of the United States Treasury under Richard M. Nixon. I know what people say about Nixon. But he didn't do nothing them other ones don't do, just sweated more. He was raised up poor, too. Down there in the Mojave Desert. You can't blame a man raised up poor."

He could have driven us anywhere. We weren't watching the road.

"A cripple, too. Polio got him the month before they found that vaccine. If he'd had him some money, he might have been able to use his legs."

"Nixon had pretty bad posture," Sligo said. "But I don't recall him having polio."

Mr. Albert clucked. "Mr. Kleinberg needed help with near everything. Making water and such. I used to drive him to his speeches and afterwards he'd say to me, 'Bert'—he called me

Bert, that was his nickname—'Bert, you got more sense than that whole room put together. If you wasn't colored, I believe you'd be right on top.' He came to Mrs. Albert's funeral, too. He was in pretty bad shape by then, with the dialysis. But there he was, in a fresh suit. Set some roses right at the stone. Real nice roses. 'Sorry I'm late,' he said. 'My driver's had a tragedy.' "

We'd seen Mr. Albert work his shuck and jive with patrons. He could be a polite old Negro, humble and eccentric, slightly dreamy. But now, alone with two unprofitable dolts, his mind circled less flattering truths. The fellow who had managed his last show, in Atlanta, was a slippery coon. The women chasing him were moneygrubbing floozies. Arthritis kicked at his joints and swelled his feet unreasonably. I wondered what had happened to his many children.

Mr. Albert turned onto a private road and rolled past a ruined guardhouse. You might have expected something opulent, an emerald city or a coastal vista. But what rose before us was a puckered white ridge devoid of trees. Gulls wheeled over the summit and a complicated stink clung to the place. Huge machines the color of no. 2 pencils dotted the terrain. They looked to be slumbering. The Buick bounced up a dirt path.

"What is this place?" Sligo said.

"Dump," Mr. Albert said.

"Why are we here?"

Mr. Albert yanked the parking brake and got out of the car. He headed for a nearby shed. We treaded the spongy ground behind him. A black tarp shook in the wind, making a sound like a thousand tiny vacuums. Inside the shed was a hot plate and a dresser painted by Mr. Albert and someone sleeping on a cot. "Get up now," Mr. Albert said, poking. The sleeper whimpered and flopped. He looked like a huge baby floating in flannel. His pajamas were damp with burrowed warmth, his features puffed and beige. He rose to his feet with an unhappy torpor and rubbed his eyes with balled-up fists. "What time it is?"

"Time for your lazy ass to get up."

The baby looked at us shyly. In a soft lisp, he said, "Who they?"

"Them boys from the university. This is Terrence."

Sligo went to shake hands, but Terrence shrank back.

The motion called Julia to mind. I didn't know what we were anymore, but the way she turned me away made me believe our fates were twined. She told me I disgusted her. It was nothing she could control, she said. My biceps—perhaps the only redeemable feature I possessed—these had become hunks of rotten meat to her. My penis, cock, what have you, that which she had once taken into her body with such misty exhalation . . .

"Please don't say anything," she said. "I don't want to see your tongue."

There was some concern on my part.

"It has to do with your spirit," she said.

I thought probably it had to do with Sligo and his girl. They had boffed away like gemsboks and now this knocking up had transpired and I'm certain she thought about this. I was more responsible than Sligo, but I was no more employed.

Sligo and I discussed the situation. It seemed to us miraculous and not a little cruel that we'd been vested with the power to create life. And yet he insisted that his unborn child was an unchangeable good, a perfect being. He'd nicked these words from Aquinas; they struck me as dubiously applied. But Sligo was past listening to reason. It wasn't that he mistook the industry of his sperm for God's work. He simply wanted to believe in a great sign from above.

"I mean, okay, there have been more successful relationships out there," he said. "Granted."

"There have been more successful blood feuds out there," I said.

"That's my kid," he told me, frisking my T-shirt for lapels. "There is a first cause in the long chain of causes, Mikey. A rational designer. God doesn't play dice."

"It's not your body," I said.

"She can't just throw my kid away!"

How happily he bellowed. What else do we seek on earth if not a trial worthy our bellowing?

Terrence was yanking at his pajamas. Mr. Albert turned away. "We'll wait outside," he said. "Hurry up now."

The RJ Reynolds building lorded over the skyline, a stone shaft crowned by a bony radio tower. "I always thought this place was a foothill," I said.

"I smell cigs," Sligo said.

"Look down, fool," Mr. Albert said.

The ground beneath us was an epidermis of mangled packs, shiny red Winstons mostly, razored in half, the butts spilling tobacco like brown guts. There must have been billions. Sligo, who had bummed enough cigarettes in his lifetime to fell a linebacker, looked stricken. "Why?"

"Defectives," Mr. Albert said. "Sprayed with too much treater, or the paper lips onto them wrong. Sometimes the filter gets cut too long."

"Why not sell them?" Sligo said. "Like a day-old-bakery type arrangement?"

"The FDA Man got regs."

Terrence emerged in overalls, his sideburns combed out. He wore the same cologne as Mr. Albert, a sweet peppery scent that made me think of mariachi music.

We trundled down a back trail to a small clearing where the appliances lay like a sea of broken clouds. Sinks and toilets and washers and ovens, torn from foreclosed homes and cast onto the reddish dirt. Not even the gulls had any use for this stuff. It was like the Eisenhower era had eaten some bad fish and thrown up all over the place.

Terrence led us to a small warren in back. He had stashed a few objects under a tarp. These he displayed for Mr. Albert: an exquisite bread box with built-in cutting board, an antique radio in the shape of cathedral doors, an immaculate white fridge with chrome handle. Mr. Albert twitched his mustache in a noncommittal way. You could tell he was pleased.

Terrence tried to hoist the fridge by himself. "That's all right, son," Mr. Albert said. "Let these boys help you." We hauled the behemoth up to the car and spent many minutes securing it in the trunk with bungee cords.

Mr. Albert licked his teeth and hummed a tune that made him seem momentarily content. He was already composing an image for the front of the fridge, a ring of children serenading a giant goose, or a purple cow leaping the moon. We got in the car and he walked Terrence back to the shed. They moved along with a certain sweet reluctance, as if strolling some royal garden. At the door, they paused and Mr. Albert slipped Terrence a bill and held the younger man's hand in his own for a minute, speaking softly.

"That's his fucking kid," Sligo said. He was all torn up at the poignance.

"Nonsense," I said. "They don't look anything alike."

"His illegitimate son."

"He's just looking out for the poor guy. That's his thing." I told Sligo to drop it. And yet I couldn't be sure. How tenderly Mr. Albert held his hand. I couldn't say there wasn't something of a father—or our wishes about fathers—in the gesture.

The Buick struggled on the way down, skidding with the weight of our haul. Mr. Albert rolled past the Reynolds Estate and told us about the lobby, where there was a rain forest funded by tobacco money. Joe Kleinberg had come here to lick his wounds after Watergate, his hopes of greater glory petered out. Mr. Albert spent most of his time back then in the underground parking lot, "a real fancy garage," he wanted us to know. "Top-notch."

Back at his place, we set the fridge on the porch and he started in, long strokes of blue softened with cream.

We descended into the cellar. "What if we just burn the whole place down?" Sligo said. "What about that?" He was starving. We were both starving. Sustenance had become somewhat unreliable in our lives. We marched up the stairs with a divan punching welts into our arms. "We could eat the dog," Sligo said.

I didn't mind the starving so much. It was only that particular meals came to mind, which Julia and I had conceived in her bed, ravenous and rashed from copulation. Roast duck in a blackberry glaze, scallops sautéed in scallions and butter, pork chops under broiled goat cheese, garlic potatoes, Maryland crab cakes, braised shrimp in black bean sauce. We couldn't cook but we could imagine. The great stupid hope of imaginers.

And what of the spoons of peanut butter? The saltines? The old soup kits and cheapie pastas that fueled our exertions? These were hard to dispute. But we were under the spell of some deeper human hunger. And it wasn't sex, though I wanted dearly to believe it was. Sex was the easy part, compared to devotion.

Up and down those stairs we went. The sun draped a shadow over Mr. Albert, bent to his task. For a few hours there, muscle-wrung and panting, we reached the end point of all concerted labor, which is forgetting.

Then a string of firecrackers went off and dusk snapped like a flamenco dancer and the smell of barbecue—molasses, vinegar, smoke—came up against tar.

Sligo dropped his end of the wardrobe on the lawn and said, "Who was that guy—Terrence?"

Mr. Albert kept his eyes on the fridge, where a flying elephant swooped over a woozy skyline. "Terrence a good old boy," he said.

"Yeah," Sligo said. "Yeah, I was just wondering if he's a relative. Or whatever."

"He got an eye, don't he?"

Sligo started to say something more, but Mr. Albert tapped the water jar with his brush, like a conductor calling for silence. There was a tense pause. Then Mr. Albert took up his brush again and we lay on the lip of the lawn and let him talk. He needed some undiscriminating listeners. That was the message. He'd set himself apart from his own people for sad, unspoken reasons and found genius late in life and now he had a little money and too many bidders. His bones ached with the mistrust.

I yearned for sleep, a sleep populated by Mr. Albert's bright winged figures. There was nothing boastful about his art. But I was too hungry for sleep. "We've got to eat," I moaned. "It's like knives scraping my stomach."

Sligo closed his eyes. "Please, Mikey. You should know better."

For a second, I was confused. Then the connection hit me—his girl had scheduled her procedure for the following week.

He pushed himself off the grass. "What about that crib?" he called out. "The one you were doing this morning. Are you going to finish that?"

Mr. Albert blinked. "It's on the porch."

Sligo joined him and hunched over the crib. I could see him watching a child sleep, a little girl, around Christmastime, that red tinselly light. This was all speculation; something between hope and clairvoyance.

"There's no central figure," Sligo said.

Mr. Albert glanced over. "Ain't done yet."

"What's going in the middle?"

Mr. Albert shook his head.

"You don't know?"

"If I knew," Mr. Albert said calmly, "I'd have done it already."

Sligo looked positively distressed. "When will you know?"

I could see where this was going. I leaped up and nearly swooned from dizziness. "I think I need to eat something. Like, now."

The two of them watched me wobble. "Sorry, boy," Mr. Albert said. "When you get to be my age, sometimes you forget. Everything happens the same. Just slower. We can go see Mr. Gabriel."

Mr. Gabriel had a place on Ninth within walking distance, next to Braxton Funerals. The marquee read SPECIAL THIS WEEK: HEADSTONES! REAL MARBLE! AFORDABLE

ON LAY WAY! Little girls across the street chanted to the thwack of a jump rope. Their legs scissored with obscene grace. Not far away, the captives of a kennel called Pit Bull City made noises of joy and murder.

Everywhere the smell of barbecue perfumed the dusk. Mr. Gabriel presided over a smoking barrel in the parking lot. The end of his nose looked like it might have melted a little in the flames. We waited forty minutes before he would allow us at his ribs. There was a six-hour minimum on each set. The meat fell away in hanks. We stood in the lot, gasping at the succulence, scraping our teeth across the bones.

"Dessert inside," Mr. Albert said. He gestured to a structure we had taken to be abandoned. We swung the door open. A few regulars sat at the counter, dipping into their drink like buzzards. The rest of the place was a wreck of stools and frying equipment and dead TVs. It had been a nightclub way back when, to judge by the photos high on the peeling walls, which showed Mr. Gabriel blasting a trumpet, his hair electrified. His sole vocation now was ribs. One of his grandchildren brought us spiced beans with turkey tails, and a lemon Bundt cake that dissolved on the tongue. All I could say was God this and God that. Sligo stopped eating, but I just kept going.

On the way back, Sligo told Mr. Albert that he wanted to buy the crib.

"You what?" Mr. Albert squinted.

"I'm having a baby," Sligo announced. "My girlfriend is." To hear his conviction, you would have thought he was Augustine under the fig tree, reciting Paul's epistle.

Mr. Albert scratched at his painter's cap. "You going to have a baby?"

"Yessir," Sligo said. He hiked his pants.

I thought about that young lout Augustine settling down beneath the fig tree and reading the words that redeemed his life: *Let us walk honestly as in the day; not in rioting and drunkenness, not in chambering and wantonness.* Sligo was after just such a transformation. He wanted Mr. Albert to find him worthy. But Mr. Albert was just a lonely old guy who painted junk. Judgment wasn't his deal. "Can't give you that crib," he said. "It's spoke for."

"Can't you make another one?"

"Sure. I can make you another one."

"No," Sligo said. "That's the one I want. The one on the porch." His voice was pinching up again. "I've got a plan."

Mr. Albert clucked. "You want to make God laugh, son?"

Back at his place, he peeled off two ragged twenties for each of us. Sligo wouldn't take his. He stared at the unfinished crib like a cow. "Please," he said. "This is something I *need*." He was talking now about things that might have been.

I tried to steer him away from the crib, but he threw me off like tissue.

"He admires your work," I explained.

"You're the one who preaches it." Sligo wheeled on Mr. Albert and staggered toward him. "Never throw anything away."

Mr. Albert cocked his head. He didn't know what Sligo meant, exactly. But he could see the larger picture, that my friend wanted to enlist him in some sad foolishness. He took Sligo's shoulder in his hand and spoke slowly. "I've thrown plenty away, son. It ain't the throwing away that does you in." He looked sympathetic but not the least bit convinced. You had to remember then that he was a father, that he understood children, their tantrums, their scorn, the stubborn imperfection of them.

Night had come now and all our illusions stole off like thieves. Julia would cast me out, sensibly enough. Sligo could see his due coming, and he looked cracked in half. We left Mr. Albert alone with his wood and his paint and his history, though he went back inside his house and chose, this night, to look at TV.

Sligo grabbed his own shoulders and shook himself. "If she could see that crib . . ."

"He'll make you another one."

"It'll be too late, Mikey."

He was right. He was right.

I wanted to believe there was something redemptive in Sligo's grief, some true desire to extend himself beyond the glamour of his wishes. But I didn't know. It was one of those situations. Augustine would have known what to do, maybe. But we could only read him. We couldn't *be* him.

The dark slid by and the lamentation of dogs faded into air conditioners. We had turned a corner from the world of black people into the world of white people. I thought about all those appliances scattered on the ground. Only a few would be resurrected under Mr. Albert's brush.

A yuppie from the Mill condos jogged past, shoving an elaborately engineered stroller. The kid's head lay still in its bedding, pink and blank. Sligo didn't seem to notice.

"That's my kid inside her."

"I know," I said. "I'm sorry, Slig."

It would be a long while before we worried this subject again. And though later that night Sligo spent every penny of our earnings on cognac and failed tomcatting and later still tore up an entire roof of shingles trying to break into his girl's apartment, until the police arrived—at that moment all he did was let his head fall upon my shoulder.

"I could still convince her, Mikey. It's not too late."

"I know," I said, though I didn't. I was just trying to believe him. It was what anyone would have done with him there weeping.

NOT UNTIL YOU SAY YES

BECAUSE OF FINANCIAL DIFFICULTIES brought on by the mis-behavior of her two sons, as well as her own unfortunate habits, Sophie Didasheim had taken, at the age of sixty-seven, a part-time position with the Transportation Security Administration at Logan Airport. She checked IDs in Terminal C. The pay scale was $9.75, a buck more for holidays and peak hours, because everyone was in a foul mood. Well, fine: she was in a fouler mood.

"I'm tired. I feel like someone walked all over me . . . I don't want to hear about it . . . Go that way. No, *that* way."

The Chinese she had no patience for—the polite questions and plastic bags crammed with Dial soap, the dizzy grandpas staggering through the scanners.

"*That* way," Sophie said. "Picture ID. *Picture. ID.* Fine dear. Go. *Move.*"

As a girl, she had considered ushers glamorous, but her ideas about life had yellowed one by one, like old movie posters. Four decades of Tareytons had turned her voice into a soft growl. The babies, at least, she liked. Cute. They hadn't been turned into goons and sluts yet.

"Hello, Dolly!" she would say. "Isn't she a princess? Look at that face. Very pretty."

She made these assessments without hesitation or emotional restraint. They were babies. You loved them. You had *permission*. She stuck her big nose into their faces and flapped her lips at them and breathed in their sweet baby stink. The parents, standing by with the paramilitary strollers, beaten into drowsy lumps—what were they going to say?

Her place in Chelsea was just down the street from the railroad apartment where she had been a young wife and mother, the central recipient of male trouble. She was alone now, drank tea laced with whiskey and lay sleepless in the new silence. Brazilians had moved into the neighborhood. The women dressed trampy and got fat. The men parked their trucks in the street and left the doors flung open so their music could bang the air around. It wasn't the same.

She worked next to whomever, mostly blacks, black girls with their queenly butts and french fries, their private language of contempt and disappointment. Shirlanetta. Deshonda. Laylani. And Raúl, her favorite, a sweet Filipino boy who made googly eyes at attractive male passengers, bit his knuckles, this kind of thing. What a pair. They ate lunch at Famous Famiglia. Raúl said she was a fag hag.

IT WAS THE DAY AFTER CHRISTMAS and Sophie was in no mood. She'd drunk a bit too much the night before, down at Mohegan

Sun. They had a floor show—some kind of winter corn ritual—and the free nog drinks. Her friend Phyllis Banaszak wanted to play craps, it was more social, she had a formula. Sophie said, "What? I don't talk to enough people?" She dropped five hundred playing Caribbean stud and spent midnight tumbling through the shops in her FRIEND OF THE MOHEGAN Windbreaker. This is what she did now that her sons were no longer in state, the bums, the no-goodniks.

"You look like ten pounds of shit in a five-pound sack," Raúl said.

"Suck a penis," Sophie said.

"*Another*?" Raúl said. "I couldn't possibly."

The lines ran past Dunkin' Donuts, all the way out to the hideous gravity sculpture. All morning the passengers trudged at her, weighed down in gifts, stupid and impatient. Their tongues smelled of coffee and Nicorette.

"*That* way," Sophie said. "Picture ID. Fine dear. Go."

Her hair was an ashy, frizzled white, lacquered into place and showing pink at the crown. The belt of her uniform divided her belly into matching loaves. She was past vanity. Menopause had flushed it out of her system. She said the things she said; to herself, out loud—it didn't matter.

"What kind of name is that? How do you pronounce that?"

"Show me your license, dear. Hold it up. *Up*."

"Palm Beach, huh? Lucky you."

Sophie scratched at her nose. Her older boy, Jay, had ducked out on a number of debts and drifted down to Florida to sell phone cards. Where? She had no idea. Some basement, some swamp. Stevie was in Huntsville, Alabama, at last report, courtesy of the county. His public defender—she sounded maybe twelve—said it could have been worse, the other driver had suffered no permanent neurological damage.

Sophie herself didn't fly. The casino shuttles ran twice a week. That was enough for her. Raúl had his Santa hat on, with

SEASON'S BEATINGS on the trim. It had to do with his kinky sex practices. Ho-ho-ho.

"I'm worn out," she told him. "I'm tired, you hear me?"

THE KID WAS TEN, ELEVEN, dressed in a shiny green sweat suit. His dad was hovering behind him, asking all the loud divorced-dad questions.

"You got your snacks, right K?"

The kid stood there miserably while Dad did the big public hug.

His ID card was from a recreational sports league. Kenneth Hodges. Lived in Los Angeles. He was four feet nine inches and a hundred pounds. Mousse in his hair and bulky braces, as if he were sucking on a bullet.

"You play a sport?" Sophie asked.

Kenneth Hodges looked off to the side, like she was such a dingbat.

"What sport?"

"Hockey."

"A stupid game," Sophie murmured. "Skate around punching people. Senseless."

"Are you *done* yet?"

"Go. Go be a pill."

Kenneth Hodges skulked through the metal detector and was gone.

"Who plays hockey in Los Angeles?" Sophie demanded, of no one in particular. "What happened to roller-skating?"

She could remember bringing the boys to the rink on Pearl Avenue, watching them whip around the scabbed wood, drunk on motion. Stevie had fallen once and cut his chin. The blood had sent him into a storm of tears. Those hot cheeks! That blessed laughter! She spent the rest of the morning humming lines to an old song: *I got a brand new pair of roller skates, you got a brand new key.* She did a dance step in her white shoes. "You're *such* a drag queen," Raúl said.

AT ONE, Sergeant Ladd pulled her off the line. He was former army, everything barked, like he was still on Hamburger Hill. "Need you for a special detail, Soph. We got an unescorted minor. Kid missed his flight."

Sophie tried not to hate black people in public. It showed poor breeding. "So? Let the airline take care of that. Get someone from liaison."

"The holiday." Ladd scratched behind his ear and peered down at her with his dark, nervous eyes.

"What about my slot?"

"Just sit with the kid. Act like his damn grandma."

Raúl stood back, doing a pantomime of Ladd swinging his dick like a lasso.

Sophie found Kenneth Hodges in one of the white rocking chairs past Gate 15. He was staring at the sleet pelting down on the planes.

"Missed your flight, huh?"

Kenneth Hodges juked his shoulders. His face was thin and lonesome.

"Tough luck."

Kenneth Hodges said nothing. Outside, the clouds heaped like slag. An elevator opened to reveal a crumpled matron in a wheelchair. At the shoeshine stand, an executive dozed on his throne while an old black man worked to make his loafers glare.

"When's the next one?" Sophie said.

"Five something."

"This gate?"

"No, actually, it's all the way across the airport. I just like the view."

"A smart-ass," Sophie said. "Just keep your mouth shut and I'll do the same thing." It didn't make sense; the kid was old enough to sit by himself.

Kenneth Hodges kept dipping into a bag and fishing out candies, then clawing at his braces. The sound was like a chicken pecking at corn.

"How about a toothpick?" Sophie said. "I'm buying."

"I made a *deal* to miss my flight," the kid said. "I told them my grandmother worked in the airport."

"Is that so?"

"Got a big-ass voucher, too." The kid shot her his grin, like he'd just invented uranium.

"How much you get?" Sophie said tiredly.

"Three hundred. Plus lunch."

She clicked her tongue. "Day after Christmas, Boston to LA. United overbooked by 10 percent, at least. And all you got was three?"

"Plus lunch."

"Show a little patience, they go to six, maybe seven hundred."

"I did wait!"

"I've heard of flights where they offered a thousand."

"They were closing the plane!" Kenneth Hodges said. He was present now, fully absorbed in his hatred.

"I'm gonna get coffee," she said. "You want something, Mr. Big Shot?"

KENNETH HODGES HAD ENOUGH electronic equipment to spy on the president: games, music, video contraptions, a dozen ways not to be where he was—but he'd forgotten his adapter. It was his father's fault. He related the story in a series of indignant grunts.

"You think I care?" Sophie said. "Go play with a piece of string."

She was thinking about Jay, his last visit, two Thanksgivings ago, how he'd sat on the couch cradling his newest gadget, peering desperately into its tiny blue horizon. She thought about the hand she'd lost the evening before, three kings, a big-money hand, the one that was going to turn her luck around, but the Chink dealer pulled a straight. Apologizing with his big teeth. It was insulting.

"You shouldn't be mean to me," Kenneth Hodges said. "I'm a kid."

"Tell it to the judge," Sophie said.

Kenneth Hodges murmured a few swear words.

"Nice mouth," she said. "Have it bronzed." It was something her mother used to say, down at the Saugus pier, where the fishermen pulled hideous speckled fish from the muck. Sophie put her feet up and groaned.

Kenneth Hodges wanted to know if she had ever caught any terrorists.

Sophie closed her eyes. Perhaps she could nap.

"You ain't seen anything," Kenneth Hodges said. He made a snorting noise her sons had made a billion times.

Sophie laughed to herself. Where did they learn such impudence? Was there a school? A place where they scrubbed away the basic wiring of consideration, taught them to snarl and huff?

Kenneth Hodges stared out onto the tarmac. Snow had begun to fall on the big, dumb jets. The afternoon light was fading. The air-traffic guys were running around with their light sticks, like it could all be rescued. Sophie retrieved from the recesses of her gums a morsel of doughnut. She wondered how long it had been since she'd baked cookies. She hated baking, all the measuring, but she loved the smell.

"You want a story?" Sophie said. "That what you want?"

"I don't want anything."

"We had one guy come through. He was a Sikh. You know what a Sikh is?"

"I don't care."

"That's like an Indian. From India. He was wearing a big white turban. They got him for additional screening and the supervisor told him to take off his turban. The gentleman didn't want to. He was going to call his lawyer. But they forced him, and you know what they found?"

Kenneth Hodges rolled his eyes.

"A snake. A tiny, poisonous snake in a plastic box."

"Bullshit," Kenneth Hodges said quietly.

An announcement came over the loudspeakers; the flight from Chicago was delayed again, which was going to push LA back.

"A snake would die anyway," the kid said. "They can't breathe in plastic."

OVERHEAD, ON THE MOUNTED TVS, beautiful anchors sang of epic weather and bloodshed. Merchants stood moribund as travelers browsed the grim magic of modern convenience. It was a terminal, a bright nation of strangers. Everyone wanted out.

At last it was boarding time for the flight of Kenneth Hodges. He was fiddling with his many cords. The gate area was a zoo.

Sophie wished him luck and turned to go.

"Wait," he said. "Okay, wait." Kenneth Hodges rose from the window he was slouching against and sidled over to where Sophie was. "Listen." He glanced at his shoes. "I don't want to get on this flight. My mother isn't going to be waiting for me. I told her I was staying over."

"You what?"

"I worked it out," Kenneth Hodges said quickly. "You said it yourself. The prices keep going up. I just need a grandma." He stared at her and widened his eyes.

"Enough already," Sophie said.

"Thirty percent of the resale value. Come on. Look at the line for standby. You'll clear at least two hundred."

"You're kidding me." Sophie gazed at the kid in his oversize sweats. His smirk reminded her of Jay, the pitches he'd made to secure candy money as a kid, the elaborate patter of the salesman asking, in his own disguised way, for love.

She was down $750 for the week, thanks to the happy Apaches down in Connecticut. She contemplated the ride home, the chill of her apartment on the day after Christmas. Kenneth stood staring at her, like Oliver fucking Twist.

"Fifty percent of face value," she said.

Kenneth Hodges let his mouth fall open. "No way. I cut your fat boss in for twenty percent."

"Not my problem," Sophie said.

"Forty percent."

Sophie shook her head. "Who are you? Al Capone?"

Kenneth Hodges kicked a pillar and cursed.

The gate agents kept calling for volunteers. The click, then the cheery plea. It was dark outside now; the shine of the airport had taken on a lurid cast. The standbys looked about desperately. They wanted paradise, the hot yellow promise of Los Angeles. Sophie held Kenneth Hodges back until they were almost entirely boarded.

She sat in her rocker and chewed on a soft pretzel, licking mustard from the foil packet.

Then Kenneth Hodges was calling out, "Grandma! Grandma!"

THE GATE AGENT FROWNED AT SOPHIE. She was some kind of Hispanic with lacquered nails. "You're the child's guardian?"

"That's right."

"You work here?"

"I do some security work, part-time."

"You realize that he wishes to volunteer his seat on this flight?"

"Yes," Sophie said. "We discussed it."

"Mommy won't even be at the airport!" Kenneth said. He clasped Sophie's hand. "I want to stay with you, Grandma!"

"Of course," Sophie said.

"I'm scared, Grammy. I don't want to go on a plane at night."

"We do need seats for standby passengers," the gate agent

said. "We can offer him a voucher for two hundred dollars on a future flight."

"You offered everyone else six hundred dollars," Kenneth said.

The gate agent looked at him.

He turned to Sophie and attached himself to her side. "I was going to come visit you for Easter, Grammy!"

"Calm down, honey." Sophie leaned toward the gate agent. "It doesn't seem quite fair," she said softly. "He's a passenger, like any of the others."

The gate agent glanced at the scrum of glowering standbys and sighed. "We'd need him to stay in a hotel for the night, so he can catch our 7:00 a.m. flight. That would mean you'd have to stay there, as well."

"That's fine," Sophie said. "My shift starts at eight tomorrow."

Kenneth flashed a big idiot grin. "Does this mean I can come back and see you at Easter, Grammy?"

"Of course you can," Sophie said.

"WE GOT HER," Kenneth Hodges said. "She was trying to be all hard-ass—"

"She was doing her job."

"—but we busted her down."

They were on a shuttle to the airport Ramada.

"We can paint Easter eggs, Grammy!"

"Knock it off, you little turd."

The other passengers were sitting there clutching their free-dinner vouchers. This was the highlight of their lives as sheep. Sophie needed a glass of chardonnay. A trough.

"Don't you have to call someone?" Kenneth said. "Like your husband."

"He's dead."

"You're a widow?"

"Brilliant," Sophie said. "A logician."

She thought, briefly, of Vincent. He had been a bum, a weak man, always coming at her with dried chowder in his whiskers. After their intimate moments, he would lie back on his pillow and put his hands behind his head, like he'd just built the Panama Canal. Then he'd talk about the Red Sox. She was relieved to be done with men, the burning need to be somehow filled by them.

"How old are you?"

"Shut up, dear."

"I'm going to get fries for dinner. Like three orders."

Sophie stared into the cold white veil of night.

"That's nine hundred altogether, three plus six, plus a bunch of meals. The burgers better not suck at the Ramada. They suck at Marriott. They taste like charcoal. I'm going to order as many movies as I want. I'll order *The Hulk* if I want. Don't you have to call *someone*?"

SHE SETTLED INTO A BOOTH at Smiles: A Lounge. Holiday banners hung from the beams, pictures of snowmen and reindeer, wreaths and menorahs. An artificial tree shed its plastic needles onto the carpeting, which smelled of cleanser. Someone had stomped one of the prop gifts beneath the tree and the remains lay there like a rebuke.

Kenneth Hodges appeared, clutching an adapter foraged from somewhere. He glanced at her shyly, through the unruly hair that swept over his forehead, and threw himself into the booth. "Dinner with Grammy!" he said.

What a miserable child. Sophie ordered a half carafe and a salad. Kenneth Hodges wanted sips from her wine glass. "Eat your fries," she said.

"They suck." He pulled out his Game Boy and began clicking away with his thumbs.

"Don't play with that at the table," Sophie said.

Kenneth Hodges ignored her.

"Who raised you? Wolves?"

"Wolves don't play video games."

Sophie snatched the game, a reflex acquired from raising boys. Kenneth Hodges looked stricken. "You can't do that."

"What's your situation?" Sophie said.

"That's mine!"

"Who's going to pick you up in LA? Your mom?"

"My mom is dead."

Sophie looked at Kenneth Hodges, but he couldn't hold her gaze.

"She might as well be dead," he muttered.

"That you would lie about such a thing."

"You don't know anything."

"That you should *wish* such a thing."

"At least I'm not old and bitter like you."

Sophie had slapped her boys when the occasion demanded. It had given her pleasure to impose a moral limitation. But she never figured out how to make them love the world, how to be kind. They seemed kind early on, but the playgrounds rid them of such inclinations. They became boys like Kenneth: fragile, trapped within themselves, their faces massacred by the blemishes of adolescence.

Sophie *was* bitter. The condition had overtaken her without permission, possibly out of mercy.

She tossed the game onto the table and Kenneth Hodges snatched it and launched himself out of the booth. She remembered that children's book, a boy prince drifting from one asteroid to the next, spinning stories for whoever crossed his path. Stevie had been obsessed with the death of the boy prince, who disappeared after being bitten by a snake. The desertion had thrilled him. She finished her watery wine. A shuttle was leaving from South Station in ninety minutes, though she knew this evening would bring only the brief luxuries of the hotel room, a hot bath, fresh sheets, someone else to clean the mess.

Kenneth Hodges hesitated at the edge of the dining room; the bones of his shoulders poked at his sweatshirt. Did he want to turn back?

No. He was gone.

THE PHONE RANG AT 5:45 A.M. Sophie answered out of instinct. She had learned the lesson of bad news, that expert locator, that tireless hunter.

"Good morning!" Kenneth Hodges said.

She had been up for an hour already. Sleep had been taken from her in her fifties. She was still furious about it. As a younger woman, she had found refuge in dreams. Now they were slipping from her, fragments, chips of paint.

Sophie hung up, then unplugged the phone.

The knock came five minutes later. "Please," Kenneth Hodges said, through the door. "You have to come with me. To the airport."

"No," Sophie said. "That is only something you believe."

"They won't let me get on the plane without you."

"Go away."

"Not until you say yes."

"Yes," Sophie said.

She lay on the bed and rubbed her eyes. Jay had been like this with his schemes, compulsive, unyielding. She had mistaken it for ambition, and invested several thousand dollars in this mistake. She got up and took a shower and ironed her uniform. Kenneth Hodges was camped in the hallway.

At breakfast, he ate: two bowls of Fruit Loops, a single slice of toast with two packages of grape jelly, half a waffle soaked in syrup, a Coke. "We can work the 7:00 a.m., then the 11:15, then I'll catch one of the afternoon flights."

"Enough," Sophie said.

"That's another five hundred for you."

"They keep a record of those coupons."

"No they don't," Kenneth Hodges said. "Nobody keeps any records. It's a separate system from the tickets."

Sophie shook her head. "You've done this before."

Kenneth smiled into his lake of syrup.

"What's the point?"

"Money," Kenneth said. "Duh. You sell the coupons online. Super easy."

"Your dead mother must be very proud."

Kenneth picked at his braces. "One flight. It's easy money. They won't let me on the flight without you."

"Stop lying. What a loathsome child."

"I'm not lying."

Sophie looked at Kenneth and he began laughing like a lunatic. He summarized the plot of the film he had watched the previous evening. It involved a serial killer who targeted pregnant women. Was it so hard to raise children these days? What made them like this?

"Does your mother know to pick you up?"

"Whatever," Kenneth Hodges said. A streak of green milk had dried on his chin. "She'll send someone."

ON THE RIDE OVER, Kenneth Hodges talked about all the things he had purchased and the things he might purchase in the future. He was adamant about certain inventions. Modern science would create a headset that allowed people to enter cyberspace for entire days. This would involve a lens that fit over the retina as well as an implant that triggered the correct brain impulses. He had seen a program on television. In the next century people would no longer be trapped in three dimensions, they would enter worlds of their own creation, meaning subatomic particle diffraction and time travel. He also wanted a motorcycle.

Sophie stared at the somber construction crews working on the roads that led into Logan, a maze of off-ramps the color of gruel. Nothing was ever done, it was always suffering some improvement. Were human beings really such factories of discontent?

Kenneth Hodges had placed tiny plastic buds in his ears. He

was speaking too loud. Sophie told him to shut up. "What?" he said. "*What?*"

He held a white device with a tiny screen, on which a man with blue hair and rivets in his face was jumping from the top of a building. The sound that came from the buds reminded Sophie of a shrieking baby.

He stepped down from the shuttle with his bulging backpack. Watching him labor under its weight made her sentimental. He stood at the curb, a little prisoner shivering in his sweat suit.

"You don't have a coat?" Sophie said. "You should have worn a coat."

Kenneth Hodges bobbed in violent agreement to the music. His neck showed knuckles of spine. "*What?*" he shouted.

SHE LED HIM through the employee line at security while her colleagues ribbed her about her new boyfriend.

"Young and tender," Raúl whispered to her. "Nice work, Soph."

"Gross," Kenneth Hodges said. "Skank-o-rama."

At the gate he stood near the window, refusing to speak to her. The flight was overbooked. When the gate agent called for volunteers, he glared at Sophie. "They're just giving away money," he said to her. "Someone's gonna get it. Why not us?"

It was like listening to the song of a gambler, that hopeless serenade she had heard so many times, had produced herself while the dealers and croupiers stared across the green and smiled professionally. This was when you knew you were in trouble, when you reached for luck, fanned at it like a smothered flame.

"You're just a chicken," Kenneth Hodges said. "We could have done this again, but you were too chicken."

"Cluck cluck," Sophie said.

She walked with him to the boarding area, but he told her to get away, he didn't need her help, so she stood back and watched him try to haggle with the gate agent. He had given himself over to deceit. His face contorted with emotion as he worked the familiar angles of pity and hope, the bright promise of what he might get away with. He honestly believed he was keeping himself safe from people.

The gate agent shook her head. It was too late. She needed a boarding pass. He pretended he had lost it, made a fuss, finally pulled it from his back pocket.

Sophie looked at his face. He was sadder than she could remember her boys ever being. Perhaps age had granted her this: the capacity to forget what she needed to forget. But then Kenneth wheeled around and looked directly at her and shouted something that brought back every wound of motherhood.

She was supposed to report for work now. It was her job to inspect IDs, to make sure people were who they said they were. But she sailed past her checkpoint and for a moment lost track of where she was—a supermarket, a casino, the hospital where she had staggered happily with her precious little bundles? Then a glass door slid open and a blast of cold air brought her back. She wanted to call her two boys, to hear their voices, to bake a lasagna for them. She wanted to hold Stevie, not in some room filled with chipped plastic benches and old vending machines, but in their home, on the familiar rugs that smelled of them, their hair and breath. She wanted to know when they had slipped from innocence, the precise moment; how she had failed them. There were so many people swirling around her. Planes rose above them all, filling the air with a painful trembling.

Later she would drink a pint of bourbon. She would take the bus down to Mohegan, or Foxwoods, didn't matter which, and settle in for the long haul. She would sit in a row with the others and consent to the wagers that weren't about money or new clothing, but simply about themselves, what they deserved. She would buy a fresh pack of Tareytons and pull the blue smoke deep into her lungs.

Forget the boy, his soft face, the terrible stab of his farewell.

"You think I care?" Kenneth Hodges said. "I never cared."

SHOTGUN WEDDING

CARRIE HAD NEVER SEEN Dr. Joel Olefeeder before, but he was the only one available under her medical plan—the old HMO clusterfuck—so here she was, at a chintzy little family clinic in the ass end of San Diego. She felt achy and tired, as if she might have the flu, the scary kind with the special abbreviation she could never quite remember. The waiting room smelled as if someone had just burned popcorn. She signed in and took a seat across from the aquarium, where a young father was patiently trying to prevent his toddler from murdering the fish.

It was a Monday morning in spring, sweltering already, and Carrie was going to be late to work, which meant her Corporate Torture Device would soon start buzzing with pleas from relentless copywriters, looking to her for the guidance and approval they should have received long ago from their parents. She turned the Device off and picked up a *Time* from three years ago. Racism was out of control. Civil war was destroying the Congo. Hollywood was auto-cannibalizing. *Time* made it all seem delightful.

The girl at sign-in called her name and directed Carrie to a patient room. To her surprise, the nurse who appeared was Delores Fuentes, a high school classmate from two decades ago. She too had been one of the fat girls who stood by, year after year, and watched the others dance. Delores was still a tubbo. She pretended not to recognize Carrie. "I'll be back in a minute, Miss Stoops."

Through a glum devotion to celery in its many enticing forms (stalk, juice, pudding), Carrie had entered the kingdom of the slim five years ago. Within months she'd been promoted and met her fiancé, Brian, though he'd recently moved to Milwaukee to open his own ad agency, a circumstance she refused to dwell on.

Carrie undressed and slipped into her paper gown. Delores returned to take her temperature and blood pressure. She wanted to confide in Delores, something like: *I'm sorry you're still fat. Being skinny isn't so much better in the end. No, I'm not just saying that.* But before she could get a word out, she noticed Delores's wedding ring. Carrie had her own ring finally, a big diamond promise thirty-four years in the making. She and Brian hadn't set a date. They had set a date to discuss setting a date.

Delores departed and Carrie passed the time browsing medical supplies. Tongue depressors. Disposable thermometers. An industrial jar of Vaseline. She plucked a pair of latex gloves from a box on the counter and touched at her face absently. The gloves were coated in a chalky film—reptilian. Was this what it would feel like to be a snake handler? But snakes weren't really chalky, were they?

Behind her, Dr. Olefeeder cleared his throat.

"Sorry," Carrie said. She pulled off the gloves. "I was sort of chilly."

The doctor regarded her quizzically. He was a large man with a swirl of hair that sat on the crown of his head like a Danish. His ears were red and damp, as if they had just been defrosted. "What can we do for you today, Miss Stoops?"

"I'm worried I might have something, like the flu," Carrie said.

"I see," Olefeeder said brightly. He consulted his records. "You don't seem to be running a fever."

"My stomach feels upset."

Olefeeder gestured for her to lie down on the exam table. He raised her gown and laid the cold disc of his stethoscope on her chest and told her to breathe. Then he set both his hands on her belly. Carrie braced for the inevitable prodding. But Olefeeder's touch was nimble. His fingers danced across her skin and he closed his eyes and for a moment let his head loll to the side, like a blind piano player.

"It's more of a general thing," Carrie said. "Almost like a . . . wooziness?"

Olefeeder's great body tensed. His fingers fell still. Then he began a delicate glissando from her belly button to the sensitive flesh at the top of her thighs.

Carrie didn't know what to do. Olefeeder wasn't hurting her, exactly. This was more in the nature of a caress. She had always suspected that blind men would be good in bed, and began to envision a scene in which she was assigned the task of leading Ray Charles to his private dressing room, which included a heart-shaped Jacuzzi. This was after a big concert. Ray was in a thin silk robe and he asked her, in that husky voice of his, would she help him find the top step, and he shed his robe right there and set his hand, his gentle, gentle hand, on her arm. And just at this moment—as Carrie gazed at his physique, the old braided muscles and smooth dangling sex—Olefeeder removed his hands and lowered her gown.

Carrie let out a little moan of disappointment, which she tried to camouflage, absurdly, by pretending to sneeze.

"When was the last time you had sexual intercourse?" Olefeeder asked.

The question brought her up short. "I'm not sure I understand. Is there something wrong?"

"Not at all!" Olefeeder smiled broadly.

"A month ago. Six weeks, maybe." Carrie flashed to an image of Brian's torso above her, narrow and thickly sprigged with black hairs, his lips peeled back to reveal pale gums. This was his *I'm coming* face. The expression always reminded her of the novel *Jaws*, in which a woman describes her lover as looking like a shark. Carrie was, she often feared, a pathetic person.

"Did you and your partner use birth control?" Olefeeder said.

"Of course we did."

Carrie had gone off the pill six months ago. She told Brian it was to minimize side effects, but they both knew she was lodging a protest against his upcoming move, and the almighty Plan that lay behind it. So now they used condoms slathered in a diabolical anti-sperm sauce that lent their erotic forays the disquieting aroma of a chemical spill.

"I'm wondering if it's occurred to you that you might be pregnant."

"*Pregnant*?"

"Pregnant!" Olefeeder said the word as if he had just hit a bingo.

"I haven't seen my partner in more than a month. I got my period after he left." Carrie shook her head. "I don't mean to question your expertise. But, I mean, what are you basing this on?"

Olefeeder nodded. "I see your point." He turned to the drawer behind him and handed her a small plastic cup. "It's really the only way to know for sure."

"But I came in here to find out if I have the flu," she said.

Olefeeder tapped the chart with his pen. "As I said, someone with the flu would present a fever, but if you want me to take a culture I can do so."

He smiled at her again with his big, well-meaning face and Carrie felt the sudden urge to shout at him, *You're not listening to me!* But she was a patient. She was wearing a paper gown. "That won't be necessary," she said curtly.

On her way out of the office, Carrie spotted Delores hovering near the sign-in desk. It was now obvious why she looked so fat—she was pregnant.

"THE WHOLE THING WAS JUST TOTALLY CRAZY," Carrie said. She was stuck on I-5, talking with her best friend, Rita, on her Corporate Torture Device and simultaneously wishing death to every other driver on earth. "This doctor just, like, felt my stomach and told me I was pregnant."

"That's so weird," Rita said. "I thought there was something different about you, like this glow—"

"I'm *not* pregnant. That's the whole point. It's been two months since I had sex."

"Didn't Brian come out last month?"

"*Early* last month. And I'm sure I got my period after he left." Carrie pictured her calendar, the sad wishful smiley faces designating Brian's visits. Long ago, her mother had urged her to flag the days of her period with gold stars, but the ritual came to feel degrading—*Great job menstruating!*—so she'd opted for keeping a mental tally.

"Okay," Rita said. "But what if you were? Would he freak?"

Carrie pondered this question. "I'm not sure," she said at last.

An unplanned pregnancy was definitely not part of the Plan, which called for Brian to get the agency up and running, then to send for her, as if she were some lady pioneer. He'd spent months selling her on the virtues of Milwaukee: the winged art museum; the downtown ice-skating rink; the breeze off Lake Michigan. This was supposed to compensate for the fact that it was freezing and had no Mexican food.

But why hadn't Carrie moved with him? That was the question her mother, with her frantic radar for discord, had asked immediately. Carrie cited the brutal hours of a start-up, her work commitments. She didn't mention her own reluctance to leave San Diego, its wild canyons and stinking marinas, the baked brown slopes of the Cuyamacas.

"Are you going to tell him?" Rita said.

The vehicle in front of Carrie—it was about the size of a space shuttle—chose this moment to stop entirely and Carrie hit her brakes. "There's nothing *to* tell him. Some quack believes I'm knocked up based on . . . See, this is exactly what I'm talking about. Just because he's a doctor and a man you immediately believe him. When I'm the one, it's my body, and goddamn Brian, he probably wouldn't even—"

"Why are you screaming?" Rita said.

Carrie took a breath and her throat caught.

"Are you okay?"

"PMS," she said quietly. "Fucking PMSing."

CARRIE WORKED AT EVANS & WINDELL, a boutique agency in the Gaslamp Quarter, meaning they worked on projects rather than campaigns, meaning they had integrity and a modern-art installation in the lobby that looked very much like a disemboweled ostrich. Most of the editorial staff—"creatives," they called themselves now—appeared to be in college. They threw gang signs ironically and texted with one hand and exuded a disheveled optimism. Every time Carrie walked in the building (art deco, naturally) she felt ninety-five years old.

She arrived after ten, frazzled and off-balance, and immediately set off on foot for the bank. Well, why not? What was the point of logging the insane hours she did if you couldn't run an errand once in a goddamn while? At the bodega, she bought fruit salad. The TV behind the counter showed a baby seated in the middle of a radial tire, burbling in a manner meant to suggest all-weather traction. The lone billboard above Market featured an airbrushed baby swaddled in a Nike fleece with the banner JUST GOO IT.

At the bank, Carrie got in line behind a woman dressed in a snappy pantsuit. Incongruously, the woman had a baby flung over her shoulder. The infant, dressed in a canary Onesie, slept peacefully. And then, right in front of Carrie, the child opened its mouth and released a gout of cloudy liquid, most of which landed on his mother.

"Oh! Diego!" The woman set the kid in his stroller and examined her outfit. "Wouldn't you know it? The one time I leave the diaper bag in the car!" The woman gestured at the baby, then, as if by some previous arrangement, at Carrie. "I'll just be a minute!" A rancid odor rose from the boy. His eyelids were threaded with tiny magenta veins. Diego? There was nothing to suggest even a trace of Latin blood. His mother—she was now, for some reason, haranguing the branch manager—looked Jewish.

Brian was half-Jewish. "The lower half," he liked to joke. He had an endearing way with his insecurity, but there was something deeply clannish in his mind-set. It seemed to Carrie that she was always being kept just beyond range by his ambitions. He could be terrifically persuasive, even charming when needed. But the word that came to mind when Carrie thought about him was *overdetermined*. His marriage proposal, though delivered at sunset on a tropical beach, had sounded like an arbitration ruling.

Diego's mother now returned and lifted her child from the stroller. "Thank you so much," she told Carrie. "You're a peach. Something must have disagreed with his little tummy. Is that right? Did something disagree with your little tummy?"

The child spat up again.

WHEN CARRIE RETURNED TO HER OFFICE, her boss was pacing. This was fine. Neil paced a lot. He was an edgy man. He *needed* to pace. The problem was that he was pacing in Carrie's office.

"Haven't we talked about this?" Carrie walked to her desk and picked up the Lucite nameplate. "It's really better that you don't come into my office unless I'm here, Neil. Unless you're invited. See, when you come into my office and I'm not here I get worried that you might be checking through my drawers, trying to find my big pink work vibrator with the special rotating clitoral cuff."

"I don't know anything about that," Neil said.

Carrie made it a point to mention sex toys, because she knew this would put Neil on the defensive, which was where you wanted a boss like Neil, whose loneliness bled into his duties and made him a tenacious oversharer. He had confessed to Carrie during last year's holiday party that he feared he would never find a woman who could love the real him, a reasonable concern. Carrie was furious that he had singled her out for this declaration. It was as if they now bore the burden together.

"I just wanted to know if you'd looked over the memo," Neil said. "The new maternity-leave-policy memo."

"As a matter of fact I haven't."

"Did you check your e-mail? It's been in your e-mail since 9:00 a.m."

Carrie sat down at her desk and picked up her framed photo of Brian dressed as an elf and considered hurling it at Neil's head. "Why are you bringing this up now?"

"You're the one who brought it up," Neil said. "*You* brought it up. Last May. Remember? You said any civilized office should have a policy. That was the language you used, if I recall. I thought this would make you *happy*, Carrie." Neil was pivoting into his self-pity offensive.

"I'll take a look at it," Carrie said.

Neil cleared his throat. "While I'm here," he said, "could we discuss a new project? A moisturizer. Babyface."

Carrie's stomachache was gone, replaced by waves of nausea, one of which now rose saltily into her mouth.

Neil's chin pitted. "You don't like the name?"

"The name's fine."

"Is something wrong?"

"I'm fine, Neil. Give me a minute."

Carrie spent the next half hour bent over the toilet bowl, waiting to throw up. Was this the dreaded flu? Something acquired from little Diego? But she didn't feel hot. The only symptom was this queasiness, along with an amorphous heaviness in her limbs. On the way home, she bought a pregnancy test. Sixteen bucks, plus the shit-eating grin from the little slut cashier.

CARRIE LIVED IN HILLCREST, San Diego's coolest (read: gayest) neighborhood. Her mother had been concerned when she moved there, a decade earlier. "Everyone's going to think you're a lesbian, dear."

"Good," said Carrie, who was fifty pounds overweight and freshly dumped.

In fact, she'd bought her Craftsman just before the Great Gentrification, before the arrival of Whole Foods, with its gleaming, mortgage-worthy produce, before home prices went nuts. For ten years, she had been happily refurbishing. "Are exposed rafters really that big a deal?" asked Brian, who rented a condo downtown. She had trouble explaining her attachment. It had to do with the way the sun dropped down over the low-pitched roof, the buttery glow of her porch.

The nausea had kept her from eating much at work. But now, having gnawed through a plate of rice cakes and carrot sticks, she began fantasizing about a Philly cheesesteak. In high school, she had gorged herself on cheesesteaks. She and her boyfriend Tony Ducati would cut seventh period and head over to the Black Spot. The place was full of longshoremen, burly guys who smelled of Old Spice and low tide. There were no tables. Everyone stood at the counter, shoulder to shoulder.

You always hoped Vic was working (as opposed to Constantine), because he used six steaks per order, peeling the paperthin fillets from an overhead freezer and flipping them across the grill like playing cards. The steaks took just a minute to brown. Vic would cleave off a spatula's worth of onions and peppers from the heap at the center of the grill and slather them across the steaks. Next came the cheese, three squares of provolone laid, always, corner to corner atop the onions, like yield signs. The cheese began to melt almost immediately, to bubble and curl, and Vic delivered four or five quick strokes with the edge of the spatula, then layered the jumble onto a long roll from the Portuguese bakery next door. Carrie could still taste those rolls, gummy with juices from the seared meat and the cheese and sweet caramelized onions.

Those sandwiches had been her first idea of physical passion, the drip and warp of love, its redolence. She could taste the cheesesteaks on Tony Ducati, on herself, on their joined breath as they bounced on the blue sofa in the basement of the apartment house where his mom ran a laundry service.

Her own mother despised the very idea of a Philly cheesesteak. And she always knew when Carrie had indulged herself, always, no matter how many capfuls of Scope her daughter gurgled. She could scent a cheesesteak at twenty paces.

Grease—and all that grease implied—was now the enemy. Carrie had to remind herself. There was such a thing as self-control. She marched to the kitchen and popped a V8. The drink tasted like chilled blood.

Carrie settled onto her porch and, with considerable reluctance, pulled up Neil's maternity-leave memo on her Device. It was dreary and predictable until the last paragraph, which read: "In conclusion, I would like to cite Miss Carrie Stoops, Senior Account Executive, for initially suggesting and vigorously advocating this policy." The memo was copied to the entire editorial staff. Her next seventeen messages were from colleagues. The subject line of the first read: *Knocked Up???*

So now she would have to race over to Neil's pathetic beachfront manor and drive a stake through his heart.

But even if she killed Neil, the questions would continue: Were she and Brian finally going to tie the knot? Had she given any thought to a midwife? And now Carrie remembered the pregnancy test, which sat on the kitchen table in its plastic bag, with the receipt still inside.

She pulled a manila folder from her briefcase. Inside was the proposed ad photo for Babyface moisturizer: a toothless infant seated against a blue velvet background, pouring a bottle of Babyface onto its head. The child looked ecstatic. Carrie suspected it had been given a narcotic. On a yellow pad, she doodled possible slogans:

> *You're never too young to fight wrinkles*
> *Recommended by four out of five infants*
> *How come my head feels like a porn star's?*
> *Help! Mommy is taking 70 percent of my gross earnings!*
> *In years to come, when I have grown ugly and desperate and lonely, I will gaze at this photo and want to hang myself . . .*

It was now time for Carrie to have some wine.

SHE WOKE A FEW HOURS LATER on her couch. The house was dark. That was the problem with wine—it knocked her out. Brian used to complain early on, when he was famished for her body at all hours, though later he came to see this, the strategic glass of wine, as a useful ally in the management of what he would later describe as her *moods*.

Carrie was still in her work clothes. This was no way to feel: wrinkled and gross, with a head full of mud. She needed a shower. She stripped off her clothes and let the hot water do its soothing work and soaped herself down below with the gentle, all-natural gel that never stung. Quietly, happily, she leaned against the tile. She imagined Tony Ducati begging her to open her thighs. His eyes were closed and his shiny brow was quivering. That's how happy Tony Ducati was. For the sake of posterity, Carrie had granted him long sideburns and cleaned up his skin a little.

"Just a little wider," he murmured.

But there was an unsettling familiarity to this phrase and abruptly Carrie realized why: during her nap, she had dreamed of giving birth. She lay on some kind of padded rack in her office. Brian stood to one side in a lab coat, pasty and agitated. He was explaining something; the child was stuck. They were going to have to call a specialist. In bustled Dr. Olefeeder and pulled on a pair of latex gloves, the cuffs of which snapped sickeningly against his wrists. Then he set to work, twisting the baby like a cork. There was a loud and embarrassing pop as the child came free. She looked around for Brian, but it was Olefeeder who handed Carrie her daughter. The child was covered in Babyface.

Carrie shut off the water. This was just the kind of crap she had come to expect from her subconscious. A truly disappointing subconscious. Ham-handed and prosaic. *This is your brain. This is your brain on advertising.*

SHE AND BRIAN HAD DISCUSSED having kids. They had. But not for quite some time. Carrie recalled the conversation that took place a month after they got together, the carefree pre-pill era. They had both called in sick. She was a little frightened to make love during the day, with all that sun pouring across Brian's mattress. But the experience was breathtaking. Her own newly angled body, his body, the happy desperation of their hands.

"We should have used protection," Brian said.

"I thought you were going to put something on."

"I was, before you scissor-clamped me."

Carrie giggled. "Liar."

"I've got bruises!"

She was close to her period, pretty close, and anyway she liked this guy. A lot. She straddled him and ran her fingers through the hair on his chest and yanked the pale skin beneath. "You're in big trouble if you knock me up."

"Why?"

Carrie slumped back onto his thighs and considered the question. "I guess it might be kind of cool to have a kid."

"As long as it gets your eyes." Brian fluttered his lashes. "Seriously, we could make a beautiful baby."

Carrie gazed down at his sly, reassuring smile. She reached behind her and massaged his crotch. "I hope it gets your cock."

Brian reached up and cupped her. "I hope it gets your tits."

"We could sell it to the circus."

"And use the money to move to France. No, Italy."

"Mmmmm, I'm hungry."

There were other discussions, later on. But these had been grim and cautious, more in the spirit of negotiations. As the years passed, as they racked up accolades and anniversaries, the idea of children was quietly subsumed into the looming issues of cohabitation and marriage. These, in turn, were weighed against career advancement and logistics. Brian didn't avoid these matters. He was too clever for that. Instead he bled them of passion.

Carrie sat in her darkened home and gritted her teeth. Her breasts were tender. She wanted a Philly cheesesteak.

She had to call three times before Brian answered.

"Hey," she said.

"What time is it? For Christ's sake, it's 2:00 a.m."

"Funny, it's only midnight here."

"Have you been drinking?"

"Yeah," Carrie said. "I just drank an ass pocket full of whiskey. I'm an alcoholic now, Brian. You're engaged to an alcoholic."

"Should I guess as to the purpose of this call?"

"Aren't you going to tell me you have a presentation tomorrow? I just love it when you talk about your *big, hard* presentations. It makes me *hot.*"

Brian whistled in a manner intended to suggest his bottomless patience. "I take it Ms. Grumpy has arrived."

"As a matter of fact, no, she hasn't." Carrie glanced around the room, at her lovely pointless furnishings. "I'm pregnant."

There was a creak—Brian propping himself up in bed.

Carrie felt the fragile acceleration of the moment and thought about what she wanted, which turned out to be quite simple. She wanted Brian to be smiling. That's all. Just smiling there in Milwaukee, in his rented Victorian, with its absurdly large, claw-foot tub, in which, if they were feeling for whatever reason homeopathic, she would happily birth their child. (Welcome, my little pink aquanaut!) He could be stunned, too, sure, that was fine, that was to be expected. The smile felt nonnegotiable. She almost said it out loud: *Are you smiling, Brian?* But the silence had her a little freaked. "Is there a delay on this line?"

"Okay," he said, "okay, okay. You've got my attention. Talk to me, Carrie. Details."

"I went to see my doctor yesterday. He said he thought I was pregnant."

"And he gave you a test?"

Carrie paused. "No."

"Then how did he know you were pregnant?" Brian said.

"He said I showed the symptoms."

"So this is what, speculation?"

"I took a test," Carrie said softly. This was not technically true, but it did bring Brian's interrogation to a brief and gratifying halt.

"One of those *home* tests?" he said, almost meekly. "Why didn't your doctor give you a test?"

Carrie squeezed the phone. She closed her eyes and there was Brian with his ridiculous, sharky orgasm face. "Are you smiling right now?"

"What?" Brian said. "Am I what?" His breath rattled around inside the receiver, tense and rhapsodic.

In the olden days, this would have been the end of the line. No more wiggle room. Just a daddy with a shotgun (or a broadsword or a nice big rock) and a few witnesses and the couple themselves, the sweaty groom and the pink bride, stepping awkwardly onto the long gray carpet of compromise.

"Let's not jump to conclusions," Brian said finally. "Those home tests, what do they cost, twelve bucks? If this is for real, this is something, you know, we'll deal with it. It's not the end of the world."

Carrie said nothing, because she knew where the conversation was headed, where it had always been headed. He would talk about the Plan, which had been made by both of them. *We agreed*, he would say in that patient tone, and Carrie wouldn't argue. It was how women kept men like Brian, the catches, the mom-approved strivers.

He continued talking, managing his panic. "You'll make an appointment. That's first off. Until then, you are not to worry. Do you hear me, sweetie? Neither of us, until we're sure. Call me right when you know. On the cell. We'll work this thing out, baby."

Carrie felt her anger boiling off, and an immense sadness drifted in. Brian wasn't trying to hurt her. He was telling her the truth, being who he was. And she understood now who she was, the depth and weight of her needs, the possibility that they exceeded his capacity to give. This would mean bidding him farewell, the familiar comforts and miseries, the sweet schmuck.

She felt her heart crack, a big crack right down the side. The receiver, balanced on her clavicle, slipped free. His voice grew fainter and fainter, until it was just a scratch in the dark air. Carrie returned the receiver to its cradle.

SHE PICKED HERSELF UP from the couch and turned on a few lights, as if that would help matters. In the kitchen she stared into the bright vault of her fridge, with its radiant eggplant and dutiful tofu. Then she poured herself a glass of wine and plucked the pregnancy test from the bag on the table. She sat on her toilet and followed the instructions, sipping as she waited.

In the Yellow Pages, she found a listing for a sub shop and dialed it on her landline.

"Big Mike's," said the voice on the other end.

"You're open!"

"All night, lady."

She could hear the sizzle of the grill in the background, a warm shuffling of voices. "Do you make cheesesteaks?"

"How many you want?"

"Just one." Carrie glanced at the pregnancy test. "Do you deliver?"

"Not after midnight."

"But it's just past. Can't you bend the rules?"

"Sorry."

"Would it be possible, could I talk to the owner? Is Big Mike there?"

"You're talking to him."

"What if I told you this was an emergency, Big Mike? A potential emergency craving situation." Her Corporate Torture Device suddenly began blaring "My Cherie Amour," Brian's cheesy ringtone, and her dopey heart lurched. At considerable expense to her poise, Carrie powered down the Device. "Please," she said. "I really need this."

Big Mike sighed. Carrie could tell from the timbre of this sigh, a deep suffering vibrato, that he was relenting. This was Big Mike's secret: he was a softy. A big gruff softy in an apron. She heard him yell something and slam his spatula. "Now listen, my delivery boy, he was on his way out the door. I promised him a decent tip if he does this last run. You understand?"

"Absolutely," Carrie said.

"They got child-labor laws in this state."

Carrie unplugged her landline. She felt as supple and tingly as a teenager. Where was Tony Ducati these days? Laid out upon some worn blue sofa? In a bedroom of exorbitant mistakes? She glanced again at the pregnancy test, the invisible ring beginning to form. Or not form. How sweet it would be, in either case, to drink again from the grail of the dangerous and possible. To do just the wrong thing in the right spirit. Carrie glided through her little home, snapping off lights. Then she dumped her wine in the sink and curled up on the couch and waited in the dark for the kid to show up.

TAMALPAIS

FEATHER CAME UP TO ME just as the early dinner rush was ending. "Listen up," he said. "I've got a huge party upstairs at 8:15, so I need you to look after a few things."

"What things?" I said.

"Mostly thirteen. I'm thinking thirteen may need a little extra attention." Feather shook the hair out of his eyes. He was exceptionally, almost touchingly, lazy. "All I'm saying is, check in on her." Feather set his hand on my shoulder and stared at me for a moment with his lean gigolo face. "You'll be fine."

He was always doing this, trying to act all paternal, which I knew on some level to be bogus, though I was sixteen years old and had only a distracted mother at home, along with a "psychologically troubled" kid sister, and I was working at the fanciest restaurant on earth (to my knowledge) to help make ends meet but also to scout out the world beyond, and thus was idiotically susceptible.

"Fine," I said.

I grabbed my carafe and headed for the floor. Through the high windows, I could see the fog rolling in with the dusk, settling over the redwoods. The Hidden Home Inn was at the very top of Tamalpais. On slow nights I would sneak out to the balcony and fish a butt from the employee ashtray and gaze at the rambling homes below, where my classmates lived. Farther down the slope was our crap bungalow, a smudge beneath the fog. It felt good to be so high, at the top of something, almost dizzying.

THE WOMAN AT THIRTEEN was staring out the window. Her hair was a carefully arranged heap. Her lips protruded oddly.

"Good evening," I said, and poured her some water in the suave fashion I'd been taught.

"We're going to need a couple of menus," the woman said, without turning to face me. "I'm meeting someone for dinner. There'll be two of us tonight."

Feather was supposed to deliver menus, but he was timing his runs to the kitchen to avoid me. The busboys often ferried out the entrées, and less frequently, on busy nights, or if the shift manager wasn't around, or if the shift manager was busy getting coked up in the office, we took orders as well.

I brought her a couple of menus.

"There you are," she said. "What did you say your name was?"

"Austin."

"What sort of name is that?"

"Scottish," I said. "I think."

"Well. It's a very nice name. I'm Charlotte."

"Thanks," I said. "I like Charlotte, too. You must get a lot of jokes about spinning webs, huh?" The movie version of *Charlotte's Web* had just come out, which I knew because my sister had seen it seven hundred times already. It was the only sure way to lure her out of a tantrum.

Charlotte looked up at me. In the candlelight, I could see that she was older than I'd thought at first, closer probably to fifty than forty. Her neck had deep wrinkles.

"Because of the movie," I explained.

She nodded slowly, perplexed. "I was wondering if you could get me a glass of wine. Could you do that, Austin?"

I wasn't supposed to handle booze, obviously. But then I thought about Feather, who was up in the office by now, doing bumps off the blotter. "What would you like?"

"A glass of the house chardonnay would be a blessing," she said. "Though I should wait for George, shouldn't I? He'll be joining me for dinner."

"Okay," I said. "That's fine, too."

"Oh, Charlotte! Make up your mind! All right. Why don't you bring me that chardonnay?" She smiled again and now I could see she had braces. It freaked me a little to see a woman my mother's age with braces.

POUND POURED ME THE GLASS OF CHARDONNAY. He commanded the bar area, which overlooked the dining room. The design scheme was rustic luxury: redwood pillars with their bark shellacked, geometric skylights, a round hearth meant to evoke a Native American fire pit.

Charlotte wasn't at her table, though. She was out on the deck, a dark silhouette blowing smoke over the railing.

Feather breezed past. Before I could say anything, he sang out, "'She loves you, yeah, yeah, yeah!' You're a rock star, bro! I'm serious. You've got what it takes. Knew it the minute I saw you. No doubt." He was such a cokehead.

I waited for Charlotte to return, and brought her the wine.

"What sort of trees are those out there, Austin?"

"Redwoods," I said.

It was obvious she was from somewhere else, back east maybe. I'd lived in Mill Valley my whole life, so I wasn't too good on accents.

I asked her if she wanted to hear about the specials, but she insisted this George guy would be along any minute. Then she set her hand on my sleeve, clutched it a little. "Or, well, perhaps you could give me a preview. And then I can tell George. You don't mind, do you?"

So I told her about the specials, some kind of trout in a salt crust and lamb stew with mango and curry. It was that sort of menu, even though the chef, François, came in only on weekend nights. The rest of the time, it was his assistants, kids a couple of years older than me, who wouldn't be going to college, who had hacked-up fingers and a sullen, beaten-down aspect. About the only people who were friendly to me were the undocumented Mexican dishwashers. They grinned maniacally at everyone.

"It all sounds so lovely," Charlotte said. "George is going to be very happy, I can tell you that. You can take that to the bank and cash it, Austin."

CHARLOTTE HAD BEEN SEATED for nearly an hour. No sign of George. I'd brought her another glass of chardonnay and she'd put in an order for an appetizer, the crab cakes. When I brought them, she took a tiny bite of one and made a sound, like how delicious they were, and told me to compliment the chef. Then she asked me to bring her a bottle of wine I'd never heard of.

Pound whistled when I put in the order. "Have to go down to the vault for that one, little man." He returned with the bottle, which he handled with uncharacteristic caution. Pound was not beyond dropping less expensive bottles on the ground, just to show the waiters who was who. He had a fringe of hair that circled his head, like a friar, and a pink scar that ran from his earlobe to the corner of his mouth. The rumor was that he'd been in a knife fight with a Hells Angel back in the sixties.

"You're going to want to open this tableside," Pound said.

I explained that opening wine wasn't one of my strong suits. Pound considered the situation. "Fuck it," he said, and gingerly worked the cork out. "Feather's gonna kick himself right in the ass when he sees this tab." He smiled, and his scar smiled as well. "Don't let him anywhere near that tab."

"You think she's okay?" I said.

He glanced over at Charlotte, who was sitting with her back very straight, staring at her empty wine glass. Pound was basically a sociopath, but he was also a bartender, and therefore a good judge of character. "She'll be fine," he said. "She's got a room upstairs for the night."

"A double?" I said.

Pound passed the cork from one knuckle to the next. "You feeling lucky?"

"She says she's got a friend coming."

"Yeah, we all got a story." Pound smiled again. "Careful with the sauce, little man. That's your salary for the summer."

I CARRIED THE WINE OVER in two hands and waited for them to stop shaking before I poured. Charlotte gazed at me the entire time. I should have given her a tiny taste, to make sure the wine hadn't turned. But I wouldn't have known that then.

She took a sip and smiled without showing her teeth. "You're very naughty," she whispered to herself.

It was an unsettling moment, the way she withdrew into her own private world. My sister had started to do the same thing, especially at school, and this had led a guidance counselor to assign her to a special-needs classroom the previous year. "She's a dreamer," my mother declared, to the counselor, to me, to whoever would listen.

"Did you want me to clear anything?" I said to Charlotte. She hadn't eaten any more of her crab cakes. There was just the one tiny bite missing.

"Oh," she said. "No. No, I think George will like these very much."

"Sure," I said. "I'll come back for your order then."

It was a Sunday; the dinner crowd had thinned to a murmur. The fire was still roaring, throwing orange light onto tapestries hung from the rafters. It really was a beautiful dining room. I spent as much time there as I could, between ferrying my sister to art therapy and my mom to her shit job, which was, that summer, at the VA. The view was of the bay down below, the silver waves, Angel Island rising from the green, and the yellow hills of Berkeley beyond. It calmed me to see the world laid out like this, vast but also connected. On slow nights I'd stare at the Campanile blazing above the Cal campus and dream about the classrooms and dorms below.

I came back a few minutes later, but Charlotte was outside having another cigarette. Her napkin had fallen onto the rug. I unfolded the fabric and found the smashed remains of her crab cakes. Outside, the fog had settled in and when I looked back toward the deck it took me a few seconds to make out what I was seeing. Charlotte was leaning against the window, staring at me, her forehead a pale spot. A shiver traced my back.

I SHOULD HAVE SAID SOMETHING to Pound at that point. But I was very young and not much good at identifying my feelings. Besides, this was the best job I'd ever had and it was going to help me pay for the SAT prep course I was going to need to have a shot at Cal, and I felt, bizarrely, that Charlotte herself was a kind of test, a chance to see if I was worthy of better circumstances.

The other waiters were on to her, and gave me a wide berth. Feather had cashed out early. He was in his Miata by now, speeding down the mountain and howling along to the Eagles' greatest hits, trying to figure out where, on a Sunday night in early August, he might locate some trouble for himself.

I couldn't avoid Charlotte. Her table was right along my route to the main floor.

"There you are!" she said. "I wanted to ask you a question, Austin. Why is there so much fog here?"

"Oh," I said. "That has to do with the ocean, the pressure systems."

Charlotte hummed her fascination. Half the bottle was gone.

"It comes in off the ocean and gathers in the valleys."

This made no sense whatsoever—we were at the top of a mountain—and I was a little disappointed in myself. My head was crammed with facts about Mount Tam, because like every other child in Mill Valley I'd spent most of elementary school scrawling reports on the subject. I knew that Tam was 2,572 feet high, that it was home to the rare calypso orchid, that *Tamalpais* meant "western mountain" in the language of the Miwok Indians, that these same Miwok believed a maiden, deranged by love, had fallen asleep on the mountain long ago and that, if you looked very closely, you could see her outline against the sky.

Charlotte said, "If I had it to do over again, Austin, I would live in a place like this. There's something peaceful here, don't you think?"

"Yes," I said. "I've noticed that, too."

Charlotte swiveled in her seat. "I have some good news," she said, "George has prepared a party for me upstairs."

I wasn't sure what to say. The party on the second level was just finishing dessert, so I supposed it was possible, though I also knew that Tilden, the manager, would never book another one this late on a Sunday. Parties always stayed too long.

"He's going to throw a big party," Charlotte said, "based on my work performance. I've gone the extra mile, as they say." She took another sip of her wine. "It's like my father always said, Austin: hard work can take you anywhere you wish."

❖   ❖   ❖

POUND SUGGESTED I get something into her stomach, to help sober her up. Her bottle was empty.

"How was the wine?" I said.

She said something in French that sounded like a compliment.

I offered to bring her another appetizer.

"Oh no," Charlotte said. "George is throwing a big party for me, upstairs. I shouldn't eat too much."

"We have a spinach salad that's pretty light."

Charlotte looked at me and her eyes flashed with a rage so sudden I took a half step backward. Her expression quickly softened.

"The salad is good?" she said. "Well, you would know, wouldn't you, Austin? Why don't you bring me that salad, then, dressing on the side, and another glass of wine? I don't mean to trouble you, but George is throwing me a big party upstairs." Charlotte was speaking loud enough that some of the other patrons had begun to look over.

"You mentioned that," I said, very quietly.

She leaned toward me and smiled, as if we were now intimates. The wine and cigarettes on her breath made me think of those evenings when my mother would return home from a night out with the girls and wake me up by sitting on the end of the couch and ask me questions about my sister: Didn't she seem calmer on the new medication? Wasn't it time she transitioned back into her normal class?

"What do I look like to you?" Charlotte said.

I gathered myself a little. "You look like someone out to dinner, enjoying herself. That's what I see."

She turned away from me abruptly and straightened up and just sort of froze there, like a giant squirrel. Then, from the back of her throat, a wet hissing emerged.

"Okay," I said. "I'll bring you that salad, then."

❖　❖　❖

I SET DOWN HER SALAD. We were half an hour from closing. The room had emptied.

"What's all this?" Charlotte said sharply. "On top there?"

"Those are roasted walnuts and some gorgonzola."

She picked up her fork and poked at the cheese.

"You don't like gorgonzola?" I said.

"You know I don't like gorgonzola!" she said. "Don't start to pretend now, Austin. I find it very insulting." She whacked the edge of the plate with her fork and the room fell silent. "Go," she murmured. "Take it away."

I came back with a plain salad.

"Where are the walnuts?" she said.

"I was going to put those on the side. With the dressing."

"What sort of games are you playing here, Austin? Are you trying to take advantage of my good nature?"

"No," I said. "I just thought you wanted a plain salad."

"Well. You certainly are doing a lot of thinking tonight, aren't you? And where's my glass of wine? I ordered a glass of wine, did I not?"

Pound had told me to cut her off. "The bar closes early on Sundays. I'm sorry."

"That may be so," Charlotte said, "but you should know that George is throwing me a party upstairs, a very *big* party. So you should factor that into your thinking, Austin, in regards to the bar and the other matters we've discussed." She picked up the empty bottle of wine and turned it over and let the remains drip over her salad.

It was clear there would be a scene if she didn't get her wine. So I went back to the bar and waited for Pound to duck out for his cigarette and poured her another glass, a small one. Then I waited for Charlotte to go smoke *her* cigarette, and left the wine.

IT WAS POUND WHO FOUND ME, hiding out in the supply room behind the bar.

"We got to clear the main room," he said. "Don't let her freak you out."

"She's not freaking me out."

"She's freaking you out," Pound said. "I'm telling you: don't let her." He ran a hand over his pate, as if there was still some hair to clear away. "Just let her run down. She's almost done. Then we can get the hell out of here."

"Right," I said, psyching myself up. I went to clear the last few tables.

"Austin," Charlotte called out. "*Austin!*"

She looked up and smiled and began asking me all these questions. Did I plan to go to college? What did I plan to study? I answered her dutifully, like the scholarship boy I hoped to become. UC Berkeley. Electrical engineering. I mentioned my special interest in laser optics, which was the kind of thing college interviewers loved. I didn't mention my mom or my sister, how much I loved them, how trapped I felt by them. Charlotte nodded absently.

"Did I tell you about the big party upstairs?" she said. "George organized it for me. But it looks like the restaurant is closing."

"Yeah, we close at ten on Sunday."

"That doesn't leave us much time," she said. A moment passed. "Do you think I'm crazy, Austin?"

"I don't, actually," I said.

"Do I look crazy to you?"

"No, ma'am." I shook my head. "About the party, though, is there some chance you might have gotten the date confused?"

Charlotte pulled a large leather purse from beneath the table and removed a tattered date book. She began riffling its pages and nodding to herself. She closed her eyes and let her fingers glide across the tiny black numbers, as if reading Braille. Inside the purse I saw a thousand torn postcards and twenty-dollar bills.

❖   ❖   ❖

CHARLOTTE WAS THE ONLY DINER left at closing. Pound had sent the last waiter home, the cooks were history, and the overnight crew had arrived, cursing in Spanish. Pound was getting ready to do stock.

"I'm going to need some help with the check," I said.

He took the slip, made a few swipes, and handed it back to me. The tab had come to more than nine hundred dollars, thanks to the wine. I stared at the figure and my hands began to shake again. That seemed an awful lot of money to ask for, from anyone. Pound went back to his inventory, but I stood there until he had no choice but to turn around.

"You don't want to do this, do you?" He leaned over the bar and fixed me with a look, somewhere between pity and disgust. "Okay," he said. "Calm down, little man. I'll handle it."

"Thanks," I said. "Thanks."

Pound headed out to the main floor. He stood talking to Charlotte. She twisted her napkin and let out a series of little sighs. Pound crouched down, so they were face-to-face. There was something both gentle and bullying in the gesture. She began rooting around her purse, pulling out twenties and piling them beside her salad. Pound took the money, talking to her the whole time in a low tone. Then suddenly Charlotte shrieked at him. Her voice echoed in the silence of the room. Pound held his hands up in front of him and slowly backed away.

"What was that about?" I said.

"Don't worry about it," he said.

"Is she going upstairs now?"

"That's the thing," he said.

"What's the thing?"

"She wants you to escort her to her room."

"Oh no," I said. "No way. I had to deal with her all through dinner."

"Yeah," Pound said. "And you got paid for that. That's the nature of what you're involved in. It's called a job." He tossed a stack of twenties onto the bar.

"What's this?"

"Your tip."

"How much is it?"

"About five hundred bucks, that would be my guess."

"I'm not taking it," I said. "We can put it in the night kitty. It's an orphan tip."

Pound grinned. "A real humanitarian, huh? Listen, you handled the table. Am I right? Isn't that what you just told me?"

"It was Feather's to begin with."

"Feather," Pound said. "Jesus H. Christ." He gathered the money into a neat stack. "You earned that tonight, understand?"

"I don't want it," I said.

"You can decide when you get back."

"I'm not going to do it," I said.

"Yeah you are. You're going to go over there and do your polite-young-squire routine and walk her up to her room. That's what you're going to do. Because the other solution is for me to call the police, and I don't want to do that, and you don't really want me to do that, either." Pound sighed. He glanced at me and touched at his scar. "She's just a lonely broad in her cups, okay? Don't turn it into something it's not, little man."

CHARLOTTE WAS GLAD TO SEE ME. She had been staring at her wine glass. "Austin," she said. "We must stop meeting like this." She nodded toward the bar. "Is that man your boss?"

"Sort of."

"Bosses can be rather difficult to discipline, can't they? I think it might be time for me to retire for the evening."

"Yeah," I said. "I could show you to your room, if you want."

"That would be enchanting."

She'd made a mess of her place setting. There were crumpled tissues everywhere, bits of food, lipstick smears. It made me think of my sister's room: the wreckage of a mind exploding.

Charlotte stood, a little uncertainly, and hooked her arm in mine, as if we were all set to embark down the Yellow Brick Road. She stopped to look at everything: the yellowed antlers above the hearth, the assembly of Miwok bowls in the reception area, the stained glass windows. She had questions about all of this stuff.

At one point, she leaned against me and I felt the small bones beneath her blue blouse. The top few buttons had come undone and most of one breast was visible, puddled atop the underwire.

I was worried she might want to kiss me. Or that she'd invite me into her room for a nightcap. She'd given me this huge tip, after all. Maybe this granted her certain rights. I didn't quite understand what she was after, that she wanted not to be alone, that this desire was itself scarier than anything my young mind could have dredged up.

We climbed the staircase, with its thick pile carpeting. Charlotte knew her room number, but she didn't have her key. Down I went, to the reception desk, where Pound was waiting. He handed me the spare without a word.

Charlotte fumbled with the key for a minute before turning to me. "Would you mind terribly, Austin?"

I opened the door and stepped back. "Well," I said, "it was a pleasure making your acquaintance."

"Thank you," she said finally. "You're certainly a young man of outstanding promise. I saw that right off the bat. You are going to go places in this world. I don't mind saying so."

She stepped toward me and I flinched, just a little, enough for her to see that I was petrified. Her smiled collapsed and her face became engaged in a sustained struggle to not further alarm me. "I expect great things from you," she said, haltingly. "Great things, Austin."

"Yes, ma'am," I said.

She leaned forward and kissed my cheek. The tip of her nose remained against my neck for a moment and she inhaled deeply, as if to breathe in my youth. Then she stepped back and gazed at me, her eyes captured in small sorrowful rings of mascara. "You're going to leave me now, aren't you, Austin?"

For a few awful seconds I stood there, pinned beneath her need, my heart ripping away. "Yeah," I said. "I am."

POUND HAD A DRINK WAITING FOR ME. I drank, then coughed.

"You did good," he said. "Don't sweat the details. That's what the world does to some folks. Take your money. Buy your mom something nice."

"All right," I said. "*Fine.*"

I stuck the money in my sock and went out to the deck to clear my head for the ride home. The fog was always heaviest in summer. I took a last sip of my drink and hurled the glass over the deck and watched the fog swallow it up. I thought I heard footsteps behind me and all at once I had the strangest feeling: that if I turned around, my sister would be standing there in the dark, wanting something—a juice box for her pills, an airplane ride, another hug—even though I knew she was asleep by now, her tireless body at rest in some impossible position. But when I turned, no one was there.

I ran to get my bike. The trip down Tamalpais was my favorite part of work, my favorite part of life, really: coasting the insane curves of Route 1 with the wind ringing in my ears and the redwoods zooming past. The booze hit me about halfway down, and the simple relief of having survived Charlotte, being free of my labors and not yet at home—all this left me elated.

I didn't know what was happening above. I would only hear the story later, from Pound: how Charlotte got up in the middle of the night and prowled the halls of the inn in her undergarments, whacking her purse against the walls; how the police showed up and forced her to return to her room; how, at dawn, she walked to the nearby fire station and smashed two windows.

Pound regaled the rest of the night staff, loud and cavalier, another loony bird for the files. But when it was just him and me alone, later on, he sounded haunted.

"You know about my binoculars," he said.

There was one particular spot on the rear deck that offered a clear view into the second-story rooms. He'd been curious what Charlotte would get up to after the police left, so he looked into her darkened room and suddenly the light snapped on and Charlotte was lying on her side, on the bed, her hands clasped beneath her cheek in a posture of prayer.

"She had this black mask on and she was staring straight at me," Pound said. "She knew I was there, little man. She reached out her fucking hand. Then I realized she wasn't wearing a mask at all. Her mascara had run with tears."

I didn't know any of this as I whizzed down Tamalpais on my bike. Up above, Charlotte might only have been a lovesick maiden sleeping peacefully on a mountain. If I'd turned and squinted, I might have seen her outline against the sky. And down below, there was me, a boy plotting his escape, the getaway dough tucked in his sock.

It was a warm night and I was building up speed on the straightaways. I remember thinking at one point that I'd need to brake if I wanted to stay in my lane, because a sharp turn was coming up. But I was feeling too good to slow down. It was nearly midnight and the only thing I could see was my headlight cutting through the milky fog and for just a second I no longer felt like a thing made of flesh and bone. I was a beam of light: ecstatic, weightless, invulnerable. I veered into the wrong lane at thirty miles per hour, waiting for the car to appear in front of me, which would mean the end of my life. A single wrong turn in the fog—this was the dark velocity of madness, and it seemed to me, in that single second, perfectly natural, perfectly human.

WHAT THE BIRD SAYS

JIM CUTLER HAD FLOWN DOWN TO ASHEVILLE to be there while
his father died but it was taking longer than expected so they'd
given the old man morphine. Now he was seeing things. "Not
things," he insisted. "A bird."

"What kind of bird?" Jim asked.

"How the hell should I know? A bird, damn it. With wings.
And a beak."

The old man scowled at Jim, while his other children, the four
daughters, pitter-pattered down the hallways of the Cutler estate, whispering tragically and getting in the way of the nurse
and consoling their mother, who did not require consoling so
much as a mild barbiturate. This is what the bird said.

They had his father downstairs in the snuggery, with its

carved walnut panels, where he had once taken brandy with the governor, and where he now took plasma and 5 percent dextrose through an IV. He was propped in one of those mechanical beds, still dressed like a man of wealth. But the elegant cuffs and tabbed collars merely emphasized his frailty. His clothes had begun to mock him.

Several years back, the old man had suffered a heart attack, which had deadened a significant portion of the muscle. The strokes had set in next. And now there was some problem with the kidneys. Everyone had expected calamity. A firebomb, a tornado. His father was not the sort to diminish. Jim had trouble looking at him, the blue eyes all watery.

The old man was no happier about the arrangement. He'd asked Jim to come down from Boston. But the request humiliated him and this humiliation sent him back into the loyal arms of rage. He greeted Jim—after five years of silence—by asking: "Found a job yet, boyo?"

The old man spat into a tissue.

Jim did have a job. He was a tree surgeon. He owned his own business, pulled in ninety a year, with a crew of six. But he had chosen to forsake his birthright as the heir to Cutler Lumber. The business stretched back seven generations, to the land grants and the Cherokee, the age before logging roads had been hacked into the forests. It had been founded on munitions, and sustained by timber interests—axes and guns, those dependable accomplices of civilization.

"I'm here now," Jim said. "Let's not argue." He was tired from the flight, frightened to see his father in such a condition.

The old man cocked his head; one of his vertebrae popped softly. He smiled and murmured at the space just above his left shoulder. This was the invisible bird. "It was just a question. Well, look at him. He has sawdust in his hair."

"Who are you talking to?" Jim said.

"He's come to kill me, anyway. Why should I bless him?"

"What's going on, Da?"

Outside, dusk had snuffed out the shadows. The ravens were settling down for the night, shuffling their wings and peering into the waning April light. The old man closed his eyes and grimaced. Jim stared out the bay window at the white oak he had climbed perhaps a thousand times as a boy. When it was clear his father was asleep, he took his leave.

The estate consisted of fifteen hundred acres, oak mostly, some hemlock and Fraser fir on the bluffs. The mansion itself had been built a decade after the Civil War, but it had antebellum aspirations: tiered verandas, rooms busy with filigree. Jim wandered them at night, feeling the clumsy grip of his history. Here was the alcove where he had savored chocolates stolen from the pantry, the closet where he imprisoned his stuffed animals, the laundry chute where he hid from the disapproval of his mother.

The morning after his arrival, Jim asked her about the vision, the bird, whatever it was. She had no idea what he was talking about. The nurse took him aside. "Morphine," she murmured. "We had to start him on the drip."

Jim wasn't quite sure how much time he was supposed to spend with his father. He had assumed his mother and sisters would run the show, that he'd be more of a special guest. But the old man had little use for the women. He'd been raised in a family of men, in a world of men, and now that he was departing that world he seemed to feel the need to settle up with the man he'd brought into it.

The old man could stay awake for only an hour at a time, so Jim visited him once in the morning, then again in late afternoon. The women, meanwhile, operated as a complex unit connected by means of linens which were to be washed, dried, folded, and tucked. He had never seen so much linen in his life. The husbands were out at golf.

Jim missed getting stoned. It was something he did a lot at home. Never on the job, which required that he hoist himself up trees and swing from limb to limb and secure knots and operate high-powered saws, but after work, when he was expected to settle down into some kind of mental life. Unease seeped into him then like an odorless gas. His legs jittered. He drank also. Whatever was in his cabinet.

"What's this word supposed to be?" the old man said. "Forty-five down." He was pointing at something Jim had written on the *Times* crossword, softly panting.

Jim leaned over the rail of the bed and the smell of the old man hit him hard. Not the burnt-onion odor of his meds, but the ancient father scent: pipe tobacco and witch hazel, the slender bite of gin, the leathery residue that haunted his desk blotter. Jim saw himself as a boy suddenly, adrift outside his father's study, waiting for . . . what? Some kind of approval, some kind of answer.

His father shook the paper and Jim examined it. "Goad," he said.

"That's supposed to be a *d*? Your penmanship is ungodly. Remember you coming home from school. What grade was that? Your mother might know. All your teachers were divorced cows anyway." The old man took a deep breath and pushed out his lower lip. "Came home with your goddamn satchel—"

"I never carried a satchel—"

"—hollering all to hell. Your mother came running to my office, holding you by the wrist. 'Have you seen this, dear? Jamie got an A.' I looked at the paper. I'd never seen such handwriting. My first thought was cerebral palsy."

This was day three. Jim had no idea how long the vigil would last. He had told his girlfriend, Samantha, no more than a week, which is what the doctors said. But the old man appeared energized by his own contempt.

Samantha wanted to come down. She wanted to share in his pain. She was a sharer, a looker-in-the-eye, a frequent weeper, a pleasantly chubby waitress at the bar where Jim took his evening meals.

"Where is she?" the old man asked. "The latest one."

"Samantha. Her name is Samantha, Da."

There was a tap on the door. Bert Banks edged into the room, rosy from his day on the links. He was married to Gwen, Jim's oldest sister. The old man had ceded control of Cutler Lumber to him, reluctantly, and only after years of assailing Bert's competence.

"Am I interrupting?"

"Interrupting what?"

"Just wanted to check in." Bert stepped toward the bed and set his hand tentatively on the rail. "You look good, sir. Whatever they're feeding you—"

The old man plucked at his IV tube, like a bum guitar string.

Bert offered a grin thick with anguish. "I wondered if you might want to say hello to a few of the grandkids. They're visiting from town."

"Good Christ."

"Another time then, Gramps. We're going to order in, Jim. Join us."

"Sure."

Bert retreated to the hall.

The old man stared sourly at the door. But then his head canted into that queer listening posture, and his face softened and took on a pained animation. "Yes, but he deserves better," the old man muttered. "Poor bastard." He was huffing, his chest going up and down, up and down.

"Who? Bert? Is there something wrong with Bert, Da?"

"Gwen," his father said. "Gwen honey, you have to try . . ." He closed his eyes and refused to finish the sentence.

Supper was held in the main dining room, under a precarious and yellowed chandelier. Prime rib from some despicable steak house with baked potatoes dry as shale. His mother presided over the nine of them in her dark frock, glancing every now and again, ruefully, at the dusty call box she once had used to summon the servants.

Bert Banks remained unflappable, a fount of corny jokes and sidelong winks. But then Gwen excused herself just before dessert and, for an instant, sorrow creased his wide red face. When he noticed Jim watching him, Bert picked up his knife and smiled fervently and said, "Who the hell wants a highball? Which one of you lovely ladies?"

Jim might have settled for something from the storied Cutler sideboard. But he was worried one of the other husbands would start talking to him about Tiger Woods, or that his sisters would ask him how he was, in that terrible tone of concern, or that his mother would pull him aside, so that they might both kneel in fraudulent prayer.

Instead he absconded with one his father's ancient Cadillacs and drove east, bombing down the dark highways of his youth, where he'd nearly killed himself a dozen times fishtailing around curves, the wind in his hair and some girl he would never see again laughing. The Smokies loomed over him. The trees were mostly pine here, some pignut up on the ridges. Just past Hickory, he pulled into a package store and mixed a screwdriver right there in the parking lot and stood and watched the june bugs clatter into one another under the streetlamp.

Years ago, he'd bought a six-pack at this same place. Upon his return, the old man had stepped out of the shadows of the wraparound porch. "You stink of hops, like a common laborer."

Jim stared at his father. The night air brought the smell of loam and mildewed acorns. "Tell me again why I should hate poor people," he said.

The old man advanced on him, his cheeks mottled. "You wouldn't know hardship if it stole your lunch money."

Jim stood his ground in the dark. He was fresh from a sophomore-year survey of colonialism, bristling with newly acquired rhetoric: *hegemony, passive wealth, deforestation.* His arms twitched—with rage or terror, he couldn't say. It was here at last.

But the old man stopped short and twisted his mouth and Jim could see suddenly the smallness of his tyranny, a man enslaved by privilege, destined to rule women and boys. His hilltop castle, with its mansard and recessed dormers, its cornices and corbels, as if he were some sort of Scottish baron. Jim tried to laugh, just to show he could, but nothing came out. The old man spit on the ground and was gone.

And now, at the end, something was happening inside him, an oracular event. His father, who had never made a single reference to an interior life, who abhorred the squishiness of psychology, was now bubbling over with—what were they, prophecies? Or maybe the old man was just losing his mind.

In either case, he'd already done his damage. Jim had dropped out of college, refused his share of the family loot, and apprenticed himself to an arborist. He fled as far north as he could imagine and tried to find a new, more tolerant family in the bars of south Boston. But he'd carried the old man inside him, that voice of anticipated failure, and taken it out on his girlfriends, all those sweet women turned mean with neglect. He thought of Sam, the soft flesh at the base of her neck. He thought of the trees where he hid during the day like some kind of great featherless bird bent on destruction. He thought of the last thing his father said to him before Jim stopped taking his calls: *When are you going to grow up, boyo?* Up above, in the dark folds of the mountain, a warbler shrieked and a second answered and then they were all going at once and then all stopped at once and the silence was hysterical. Jim missed the willows of Boston, which smelled of rain. He missed Sam.

The next day, he arrived at his father's room with a hangover. His sister Pru was taking her leave. She kissed the old man on his forehead and cranked the tiny dial of his morphine drip.

Poor Pru. She couldn't stand to see anyone in pain. As a girl, she'd wept when her dolls lost a limb. She buried them, with full rites, under the linden out back. Jim liked her best of all his sisters. She was the only one who'd supported his decision to move up north. "Go," she'd told him quietly. "Save yourself."

Pru had grown stout. She still moved with buoyant grace, but her tiny feet looked precarious. The old man watched her bustle out of the room and his face tilted up; he was listening to the bird. "Killing herself with food," he said.

"Da."

"Feels too much. It's an invitation to sorrow." His voice kept fading out.

"She loves you," Jim said.

"Loves everyone," the old man snapped. His eyes had moistened a little. "I broke her heart anyway. Broke all of them."

"All of who?"

The old man tried to fix Jim with a stern look. But the drugs wouldn't let him near his anger. "Turn the drip down."

Later that night, while the others sat in the billiard room and marinated their grief in sherry, Jim called Sam. She wept a little at the sound of his voice.

"Please."

"I'm sorry," she said. "It's just so sad. Are you okay?"

"Fine," Jim said.

He listened to her coo. She kept using the word *love*, like it was an unavoidable truth. Jim said "Fine" again, and then again. He was a shy guest in the province of her eager feelings. It occurred to him to mention his father's outbursts. He could play them off as comedy: James Cutler Sr., WASP Clairvoyant. But he knew the old man would be furious. "I should go," he said. Outside his window a male saw-whet tooted its lonely sonar.

What he needed was a little nip to help him sleep, that sherry, brandy, something. He padded downstairs and poured himself a finger of port. The light was on in the pantry and he found Pru there, nibbling at the corner of a graham cracker.

"Do you want something to eat, Jamie? A lamb chop? I could heat one up."

"No no." He held up his drink.

Pru did look heartbroken, sitting beneath the shelves of dried beans, her lovely cheekbones swallowed in flab. "Is he in pain, do you think?"

"The morphine helps," Jim said.

"It helps that you're here." Pru smiled miserably. "He was terrified you wouldn't come. He worries about you."

Jim set the port down. It was too sweet. "Is something going on with Bert?"

Pru flushed at the neck. She put the box of graham crackers away and when she turned back there were tears in her eyes. "Did he talk to you about it? Oh, Jim. I can't understand what's gotten into her!"

But it wasn't hard to see. Gwen was punishing her husband for the unpardonable sin of deposing her father. Her revenge was a kind of homage. Everyone knew, after all, that the old man had conducted affairs. For years he'd been involved with the woman who helped raise Jim's sisters, a Belgian girl named Florine. There had been others, one of whom had gotten pregnant and had the child. Jim did his best to ignore the drama. He preferred not to think of his father running around like a satyr in a smoking jacket.

Pru seemed to want to hug him—her hands were outstretched, beckoning—but he felt a twinge of repulsion. He wanted to tell her to calm down, not to make a scene. Then he realized this was precisely what the old man would have said and he stepped forward and hugged his sister so hard she wept.

The bishop paid a visit. He was the jocular kind of bishop, the kind who jogs. He took great pleasure in referring to himself, during the administration of wedding vows, as a "dried-up old celibate." He'd married all the Cutler daughters.

The old man ordered Jim to be present during the visit.

"He's a friend, Da. You two should have time alone."

"I don't want him pulling any last rites on me."

"He's an Episcopalian."

"Catholic. They're all Catholics when it comes to death."

So he stayed. It was a warm morning, officially spring. The fog burned off to reveal the green of the valleys. Scarlet tanagers were arriving from down south and the ravens released shrill complaints over the intrusion.

The bishop entered the room with a martini in his hand. He was dressed in a purple vestment with gray sweatpants. "Father Cutler," he said, in a stagy brogue. "You look like a man in need of salvation."

"Heaven forbid."

It was an old routine; Jim could see it hurt his father to laugh.

"Jamie," the bishop said. "The prodigal son. You look tremendous. Like a Catawba. What are they feeding you?"

His handshake was clammy. Jim hadn't expected that. A dry palm would have seemed godlier.

The bishop asked after all the relatives and noted that he had spoken to the doctors. *What can one do?* his tone suggested. *They're doctors.*

Having fulfilled his duties, he commenced a reverie concerning the prep school he had attended with the old man some sixty years earlier and in particular his role as class prankster. The bishop had shimmied up the flagpole, sneaked a donkey into the chapel, slipped ipecac into the headmaster's tea.

It was sweet, listening to his prattle. He and the old man had so many friends in common, so much ground to cover, that eventually they settled into a kind of shorthand—the invocation of names. *Ted Houghton. Forrest Drury. Buzz Shaw.* The dear departed, all those jolly young souls fallen into graves. The old man was moistening up again.

The bishop announced that he had a tee time and told the old joke about God and Jesus playing a round.

His father watched the bishop leave and was quiet for a time. Then he cocked his head and listened to the bird. "Hasn't believed for years," the old man said finally. "He'll take that to his Maker. Don't look so alarmed. The best clergy are unbelievers. It makes them more emphatic on issues of doubt."

"Do you believe?" Jim said. "In God, I mean."

"It's a fine notion. Comforts the wretches. The unlucky. But look at me now, boyo. Would you trust a man in my state to convert?"

"You're not frightened?"

"Didn't say that." The old man was breathing deeply again. With each exhalation, the bottom edge of his ribs pressed against his shirt. "It's a miracle," he said softly.

"What?"

"That we're born, all of it."

The next day Jim brought his father the *Times* crossword. The bird seemed to supply most of the answers. The names of Persian rivers, Roman generals, obscure abbreviations, even modern slang. There was no way the old man knew the term *phat*. Yet he must have, some part of him, because the bird was his hallucination.

Jim heard the whine of the door. He'd been arguing with his father over an especially thorny clue—summer green, seven letters, fifth letter *v*. His mother stood in the doorway. She was dressed in the sort of hat he associated with equestrian events.

"We're eating together tonight," she said to Jim. "A little company. The Tunneys. It would be nice to see you in a white shirt, James."

"Sure."

"That would be nice." She lingered for a moment, looking from Jim to his father. This was as close as she came to intimacy, this moment between silence and a small gesture.

The old man said, "What's it called, dear, that little summer leaf? They eat it in Provence."

"Chervil," she said.

The old man watched her retreat to the hall. Jim half expected that the bird would speak to his father and that his father, for the sake of posterity, would relay the words to him. But the old man only shook his head. "She wants me dead."

"You could have just divorced her, Da. We're not living in the Victorian era."

"Loved her."

"You picked a fine way to show it."

"It was complicated."

Jim was amazed at the helplessness of the word, the sense of self-pity his father conjured up. "You fucked the nanny," he said. "How complicated is that?"

He expected the old man to turn away, which he did, generally, when the conversation flowed too close to an undesirable truth. Instead he gestured for Jim to lean closer. His eyes were faint pools of water.

"She should have left, boyo. The guilt made me black with hate."

"You made a mess of things."

The old man shut his eyes. His lips were trembling a little. "Yes, love does that."

Such gruff histrionics. And yet Jim couldn't help feeling seduced. He had been taken into confidence. It was something his father had a talent for.

As a very young boy, Jim had come upon him once lying in the shade of the gazebo, in the hours after some forgotten cotillion. His red nose pointed at the clouds. Jim dropped down beside him and the old man opened one eye. With a comic noise of consternation he hoisted his son onto his chest. The familiar fumes of drink rose from his pores. "Just napping, boyo. Our secret, right?"

By the third week everyone in the house was spent. The old man just bulled on. He was wrung out, half gone to the morphine, minimal heart function, but he wouldn't die. He seemed determined to impose his will, to choose his own time.

Jim sent Sam a plane ticket. He was done pretending to bear it alone. She arrived in a sundress that made him nervous. "Aren't you cold?" he said. "It gets chilly up in the mountains." He tried to explain about his mother.

"How bad can she be, baby?"

At dinner his mother inspected Samantha openly, the position of her elbows, her manner of speaking. She gave no indication of disapproval, nor did she need to. The brothers-in-law leered while Pru fumbled to make conversation. Oh, she didn't stand a chance. Sam, with her done-at-home highlights and crumbly foundation, her careful bites balanced on the fork. The worst part was that their snobbery had infected him. He listened to Sam's chintzy Rhode Island drawl and thought of roadside fish houses. He judged her shoes.

Yet that night, as he released himself into her, he felt a pleasant sense of dissolution. He buried his nose in the moist folds of her neck and inhaled her scent and let go of everything. It was a kind of melting. Was this what the old man felt, as the morphine kissed his nerves? For a moment, in the dark, with Sam naked beneath him, stroking his back, telling him to go ahead and let it out, Jim saw a burst of feathers, a wing, the proud upsurge of a thrush.

He didn't want Sam subjected to the old man, but they were insistent, both of them.

"Wear something baggy."

"Honestly," Sam said.

The old man had himself shaved for the occasion. The flesh of his cheeks was pink and loose over the jaw. He wore a white shirt with a bow tie. One of the nurses had wet-combed the hair across his skull. He looked dapper. Even the dab of shaving cream near his earlobe looked dapper.

Sam seated herself at the foot of the bed.

"Move a little closer, dear."

The old man laid eyes on her and kept them there. He knew that women craved love, that a calm, sustained recognition of their desirability went a lot farther than they cared to admit— this much Jim had learned from his father.

"Yes, good. How do you do, Samantha? I'm so happy, at last, to meet you. Enchanted." He reached for her hand. He told her he had a secret and whispered into her ear. She giggled. "What do you want with a grump like him?" the old man said. "Look at that puss. Never too late to switch horses."

It was difficult not to admire his form. Jim was reminded of those summer afternoons when his father would appear suddenly in the back garden, a vision in a tailored suit. He bowed before his girls and danced with each of them in turn, their bare feet swept along the grass.

That was the old man. He operated like a pasha, seductive and cruel, addicted to the attentions of his harem. Then his daughters grew older, bumpy and dangerous, and he abandoned them to chase women half his age. Jim thought of Pru, bereft on her stool in the pantry. He thought of his sisters seated around the table for Sunday dinner in their frilled dresses. Each of them waiting for the merest scrap of love. He *had* broken all of their hearts, one at a time.

Sam was laughing, a rich, throaty sound.

The old man was laughing, too, dry tiffs of air. He was smiling, but there were beads of sweat at his temples. One had dripped down into the shaving cream. Jim wanted terribly to wipe it all away. "We should let him rest," he whispered to Sam.

"Jealous," his father said. "He's jealous of us, dear."

Jim woke early the next morning. Sam was curled around him, smiling in her sleep. He could see all her hopes gathered in the soft creases between her lips and cheeks. It made him sore with a need he couldn't identify. He thought maybe he would take her out to Chimney Rock today. It was the time of year that the broad-winged hawks built nests for breeding. He enjoyed watching them soar above the red spruce, while below in the pale oaks the warblers and juncos went berserk with envy.

There was a tap on the door.

"He's asking for you," the nurse said. Her shoulders slumped under a cape of exhaustion. "You should come, sir."

Jim pulled on some clothes and hurried downstairs.

"You always liked them plump," the old man said. His skin looked like parchment. He had a gin-soaked rag, which he patted on his lips to keep them from cracking. "Now now. I like them the same way. Delicious. Marry the woman. What do you need, a road map? Have yourself some goddamn kids. Do better than me."

"You should rest," Jim said.

"For what? For what should I rest? Don't be frightened, boyo. I've had my run. Are you listening to me? I don't have much longer to boss you around." He was clinging to the rail of the bed with one bony hand, a captain going down with his ship.

Jim's mother had wanted the entire family around for the end. They would each speak to the old man, say something poignant. That was the plan. It would have been a kind of torture—all that emotion bearing down on his shriveled heart.

"Are you in pain?" Jim said.

The old man nodded and wet his lips with the gin rag. His eyes shifted to the morphine drip.

"Is this what you want, Da?"

The old man smiled. His teeth looked so soft, as if the gentlest tap would knock them loose. "Please," he whispered.

Jim clicked the dial up, past the red tab.

The old man cocked his head.

"The bird?" Jim said. "Is he always there, on your shoulder?"

"Only when you're around, boyo. Command performance." His voice sounded as if it were coming from a distant radio.

Outside, the birds hurled their morning songs against the windows. Jim leaned close to the bed and whispered shyly, "What does he say about me?"

"You have a hard time forgiving." His father loosened his grip on the bed rail, sank down an inch or two.

The flesh around his eyes softened as the morphine flooded his bloodstream. The old man was gray as an old sock, weightless, his collarbones jutting like tusks. Jim listened to him breathe. Now what would happen? His father would be dead and his sisters would weep and his mother would remain locked away within her misery. We move from one family, he thought, into the same family.

The old man closed his eyes, but his lips were moving a little. "What, Da?"

"Bird," his father rasped. "Bye-bye, birdie."

It was a lousy arrangement. Jim had sent himself into exile, but he hadn't escaped. His father was still inside him and now there was this crazy bird, which was both inside and outside his father, on his shoulder, fluttering up and away.

"Listen," the old man said. "Do this, boyo."

Jim moved closer and the odor of his father's decay enveloped him.

"Do what?" he said.

The bird was speaking, but the old man couldn't quite make it out. "Yes," he whispered. "*Vvvvvvvvv*. Yes. Yes."

"What?" Jim said. "Please, Da."

His father was leaving the world of duty and bones, floating off to the other side. His vitals were dropping, which meant an alarm would sound and the rest of the family would come rushing into his room for one last stricken charade. The bird was saying something and the old man was trying to transmit this final word. His head was bowed in concentration; he was wheezing.

But Jim couldn't make out the word. All he heard was that faint hum: *Vvvvvvvvv*. He leaned over the railing of the bed and put his ear against his father's mouth. A hand came to rest upon his cheek and before he could stop himself he had laid his head on his father's chest. Such a small chest now. His head felt heavy as a stone. His father let out a sigh: faint, serrated. He wanted to tell the old man to knock it off, to straighten up and act like gods are supposed to. But this is what the pair of them had come to, this strange, gentle culmination.

His father continued to touch him, made a faint circle on his brow, ran his fingertip along the curve of his lips. Jim's neck went limp. He curled into the embrace and shut his eyes.

They were in this posture only a few moments before the old man seized up. His breathing stopped. Then his body heaved and the trees upon the mountains and the sky above those trees heaved also, and the birds flew in wild circles between heaven and earth and the air in the room smelled of nothing and of his father, who made that final sound, *Vvvvvvv*, then another, who said to his son at last, at last: "Live."

THE DARKNESS TOGETHER

HANK'S MOTHER WALKED INTO HIS ROOM and announced that she was going to supervise packing. Their train didn't depart till 8:00 p.m., another two hours. "Let me get dressed," Hank said. He was fresh from the shower, still in his underwear. She fluttered her hands to hurry him and backed out of the room.

They were the first couple to board. His mother made a great show of inspecting the compartments, which were identical. She was a creature of habit and dealt with travel anxiety by aggrandizing the minor dividends and setbacks of the journey. At last she selected a berth and seated herself at the window, patting the place beside her. "How peaceful this is," she said. "Don't these look new? These seats?" And so on. Her nose, dusted in foundation, kept to its small schedule of wrinkling and unwrinkling.

Though it was evening, the train filled up. "You'd think the airlines were on strike," Hank's mother said. She placed a magazine on the seat across from her and gestured for him to do the same. Hank watched the other passengers file past their compartment. A couple of teenage girls came and went and he glanced at them and quickly stripped away their sweaters and jeans: pale, smoothly scalloped, awaiting trespass. Wind off the lake thudded at the windows.

"But it is *hot* in here," his mother said. She twisted out of her coat. The elaborate bindings of her brassiere pressed against her peach turtleneck. In private, Hank's mother spoke with a tender urgency about the state of her breasts. When he was younger, she would stand before the mirror in her bedroom, disrobed to the waist, a glass of wine in one hand. "They used to be so beautiful," she announced. For a brief time Hank enjoyed a mysterious cachet among the older boys in his apartment complex who dropped by after dinner and draped themselves on the couch facing her room.

"Aren't you hot, Hanky? Take that ridiculous sweater off."

"I'm fine."

"Won't Nana be pleased to see you?" She took his shoulders, one in each hand, and squared them. "And soon you'll be off to college, won't you. What will we do then?" Her fingers made slow circles and Hank gently shrugged away and picked up his magazine.

Occasionally a passenger would pause in front of their compartment. Hank's mother dispatched them with an apologetic smile. Finally, the train eased forward. She sat beside him, smelling faintly of talc, her shoulder ticking against his. Hank thought of the two girls who had passed by, what he wanted to do to them. He wondered how long the trip to Toledo would last.

The compartment door opened and a chubby conductor appeared. The collar of his blue uniform pinched at the neck. His face was a creamy pink. He doffed his cap and held it before him. "Where you folks headed today?" Hank's mother presented their tickets. "Just you and your brother, ma'am?"

Hank's mother blushed. She turned girlish around men of an official capacity.

"What a nice man," she said, after the conductor had gone. She slipped her shoes off and rested her stockinged feet on the seat across from her.

"What a fat man," Hank said.

"Don't say that now. You know very well that people store fat in their bodies at different rates. He can't help the way he looks."

But Hank knew she wasn't angry, or even disappointed. She secretly approved of his passing cruelty.

Only a few passengers boarded in Erie and the teenage girls departed, laughing as they rushed past. "We'll get to spend some time, won't we? Not like at home." Hank's mother rested her head on his shoulder. "I don't know what you do with the hours. Shall we eat? I *am* hungry. Will you get the pastries?" He stood and turned to grab the box in the rack above her. As he rose onto his toes, she set her hands on his hips to steady him. "Look how much you've grown," she said.

Then the train lurched and Hank stumbled against her and she let out a happy shriek, and as all this happened—Hank drawing his knee first into and then away from his mother's bosom, she clinging to his belt loops, her forehead brushing his thigh—a third figure slipped into the compartment.

"Don't let me interrupt," he said.

Hank jerked away from his mother. He wondered how long the stranger had been in the corridor, whether he'd been watching. Hank edged past him, back into his seat. The man was busy fumbling with one of several zippers on his jacket and his eyes were fixed on Hank's mother. He had a large head of red hair and gave off a strong scent of cigarettes and sweat-over cologne. With a deliberation that suggested slow-wittedness, he gestured to the seat facing Hank's mother. She shook her head but refused further acknowledgment. Hank found himself looking forward to the minor drama of her rejection.

As the man settled into his seat, she made a show of the pastries, jabbering on about the bakery and its blind proprietor. "Have a bear claw, Hank," she said. "This man, Gitlitz, told me they were the specialty. What a sweet little fellow. He had a special cane. With a hook for opening the ovens. Isn't that clever?" The only sounds were the rustle of waxed paper and chewing. "They *are* good, aren't they?" Hank's mother reached out with a moistened finger and dabbed a flake of pastry from the fine hairs of his moustache and brought this to her own mouth.

As if in response to this action, the stranger placed a hand on her knee. "Please allow me to introduce myself. My name is Chaleaux. Nicholas Chaleaux. I hope you'll feel comfortable calling me Nick."

Hank's mother glared at his hand.

"Where are you folks headed this evening?"

Her face reddened and she drew her knee back.

"Toledo," Hank said.

The man nodded and drew a pack of cigarettes from one of his jacket pockets. There was an economy to his gestures, as if he had practiced them many times in a small space. His coat was thin vinyl disguised as leather and his pants were of a style that had passed out of fashion a few years earlier, drawn tight at the waist and decorated with neon signs, each reading LAS VEGAS NEVER GETS DARK.

Hank had never been to Las Vegas, but he knew his parents had vacationed there before he was born, in the brief era of their happiness.

The stranger lit up and inhaled deeply. His smoke swirled thickly in the weak overhead light.

Hank's mother coughed.

"Not much of a city, Toledo. You all have family there?"

His mother coughed again. "Isn't there a lounge for smokers?"

"Oh, I get you," the stranger said. "Smoke's bothering you. Smoke gets in your eyes, right? You know the Platters? All right, I'll take it outside." He turned to Hank. "Save my place, kid."

Hank's mother batted the air with her arms. "What a repulsive man."

"You want to move?"

"Of all the compartments on this train. Repulsive."

Nicholas Chaleaux *was* repulsive. His cheeks were tracked with scars and the heavy folds over his eyes gave him the appearance of a sleepy lizard. He looked untended, beyond tending. But his voice had a sly, taunting quality.

"We can move," Hank said, knowing they would not.

His mother jammed the pastry box shut. "I'll bet he doesn't even have a ticket."

The stranger slid open the door. "We were talking about your family," he said, seating himself. "Can't imagine why you'd want to go to Toledo otherwise, with all the niggers they got there. They don't know how to handle them in the Midwest."

Hank's mother said, "That is in no way appropriate—"

"Oh sure. I know, I know." The stranger made his eyes round with remorse. "It's terrible to speak like that, to have those thoughts about another human being. You're right. But the truth is I've been the victim of crime and it's turned me from my better angels. Where are you folks from? Dunkirk? Buffalo? Buffalo it is. What about that east side you got there? Full of them. The Adam & Eve, you know that place? Sure you do, all them drunken jigs hanging around outside like the sidewalk was put there to hold them up."

Hank wondered if the stranger had ever been inside the Adam & Eve. He pictured red light, a beery mist, shiny black tits. His mother turned to him and said, "Shall we do a crossword?"

"I got you," the stranger said. "No offense intended. Not to a nice-looking woman like yourself. Nor to your son. Hank is it? Fine-looking boy. He got your lovely eyes. Off to see family, I'm guessing. Grandma, is that it? A real family tableau." He traced the air with his index fingers, framing them, and flashed his gray dagger of a smile.

The stranger stared at Hank's mother in silence. Hank envisioned what he might be seeing: an attractive woman in her late thirties, hair in a chignon, conservatively dressed, but not so conservatively as to obscure the contours of her figure. She looked like a librarian of the sort Hank had encountered in pornography, a woman of violently compressed desires. Nick Chaleaux's leering inspection seemed to confirm this; Hank felt somehow implicated by it.

On those nights when she drank a little more than usual, his mother would roam the house, looking delicate and slightly unhinged. Hank wanted to rescue her from such obvious sorrow, but he was always frightened she would ask too much of him, tell him more than he cared to know. He felt his perspective tested by the stranger, pulled out toward the brotherhood of men, then drawn back to his mother, who had hidden her face now behind a magazine.

"Thing about Toledo, ma'am, they put a sin tax on liquor. Not that you'd have an immediate interest in such things. But with any family gathering, I've found, it's never a bad idea to have the option. Capone ran an operation down in Toledo. Did you know that? Over a Chinese laundry. Used to have guys rubbed out by drowning them in washers. 'Clean-corpsing,' they called it."

"Where is that crossword book?" Hank's mother rose from her seat and rummaged the bag overhead. Chaleaux surveyed the length of her skirt and whistled softly and raised his eyebrows at Hank.

She turned and glowered at him and stammered, "I don't know who exactly you think you are, sir—"

"I'm Nicholas Chaleaux," he said. "I wish you'd call me Nick. Now please don't get angry. Please. There's no need for that. To admire a woman of your beauty, you can't blame a man for that. Your son knows. See, he forgives me. Lucky kid. You must do some sort of exercise to keep in the shape you do. No question about it. Do you run? Or those aerobics classes?"

"She swims," Hank said quietly.

His mother fixed him with a furious look.

"Even better. Exercises the heart and lengthens the muscles. None of that shaking up the internal organs."

She took a deep breath. "We'd like to enjoy our ride in peace, Mr. Chaleaux. I'm sure you can understand that."

Chaleaux nodded. "Trains are peaceful. They move us like when we were inside our mamas, that same motion, what you want to call amniotic motion. Lots of folks feel that way. They get on a train and they like to enjoy some peace and quiet." His tone now was patient but oddly formal, like he was reciting a script. "But for me it's just the opposite. I get kind of jumpy. Perhaps this is on account of my own history. You can never be sure, can you?"

Hank's mother offered a wan smile. "I'm glad you understand."

"I'll maybe just tootle off and get myself something in the dining car. Either of you folks want anything? My treat."

Hank had given plenty of thought to the dining car on previous trips. His mother insisted the food was overpriced. He imagined fat sandwiches, steaming slices of pie. "Thank you, no," his mother said. She tucked a loose strand of hair behind her ear.

"All right, then. Your son doesn't look so pleased about that. But you're the boss on these things, aren't you?"

An absurd thought occurred to Hank: Chaleaux knew his mother. They had been lovers, perhaps before the brief, calamitous union that had produced him. This would explain the man's odd manner of speech. It was a kind of play, a way of working himself inside the familiar world of her indignation.

Hank's mother waited for the door to slide shut. "Why do you speak to a man like that? Just to provoke me?"

"Look, I asked if you wanted to move. We can just move."

"Don't be silly."

"You could speak to the conductor."

"And say what?"

"You know, whatever. There's some creep bothering you. Find that fat guy. He seemed to like you."

A familiar bloom rose on her cheeks. "Where do you get such ideas? Honestly, Hank."

They were past Vermilion and headed into Sandusky when Chaleaux returned. He moved loosely, his great head bobbing, zippers tinkling. The seat across from Hank's mother was layered with magazines. These he stacked neatly and moved to the seat across from Hank. Then he withdrew a brown bag from his coat and set it down atop the magazines. "Picked up a slice of pie for the kid, if he's so inclined."

"Thank you," Hank's mother said. "That was kind."

"I didn't want you to suppose that I wasn't thinking about you. I sure was. A nice mother and son like yourselves." Chaleaux shucked his coat and sat in the place he had made for himself. He wore a tight cotton undershirt and his freckled biceps bunched when he curled his arms. He had the look of a boxer gone slack. A monstrous tattoo cloaked one forearm. Hank stared at the blurry purple design and Chaleaux held it out for him to inspect. What at first appeared an octopus was in fact a woman whose eight arms held a man in a distorted posture of congress. His mouth was a tiny circle and his hair an electrocuted halo. The legend beneath read LOVE ME EIGHT TIMES in crude letters. "Can't tell you where I got that," Chaleaux whispered. "But it's a place your mother might know."

She looked at him sharply, her lips tensed.

He held up his huge palms and grinned sheepishly. "I just mean that it was a place over in Buffalo. I forget the name. Down by Black Rock. All the sailors used to hang out down there. Now don't get yourself upset. It's just a figure of speech. I only mean it's a place for adults, for the things adults do." He picked up a magazine from the seat and began thumbing through it. "Would you get a load of all this," he said, and whistled again. "What sort of youth-culture magazine is this? I don't remember there being this kind of skin in *Rolling Stone*." Chaleaux held up a picture of a thick-lipped young woman in a bra. "Is this how girls dress at your school? Lord help us."

Hank's mother cleared her throat. "I really would appreciate it if you held your opinions to yourself." She turned her head and settled into a feigned sleep against the window.

"Sure," Chaleaux whispered. "I got you." He tapped at the picture. "You suppose they're real, Hank?"

Hank glanced at his mother and did a minor shrug.

"You ever seen a fake pair? I'll bet you have. Nice-looking kid like you. More and more girls get that operation, don't they? With this new stuff, the saline. It's become like a regular part of the growing-up process."

Hank's mother opened her eyes and looked at Chaleaux. "I'm not sure what point you're trying to make, but my son and I didn't ask for you to join us or to make those kinds of statements."

Chaleaux touched his chest. He was back to the script. "Your son and I are talking, that's all."

"I don't hear him talking. You're the only one talking."

"Well now, I can't argue with that, Mom. All right. Now don't get angry at old Nick Chaleaux. I mean no exact harm here. Maybe I had one or two beers there in the dining car, just to loosen up. I've been under a lot of pressure lately. That's not your fault, but just the same." He bowed his head and his eyes disappeared behind the prominent lids. "I hope you won't take offense."

Outside, blackness hurtled past, interrupted only by the dull glow of disused grain elevators.

"It was nice of you to get that pie," Hank's mother said softly.

"It's important to be kind, I think," Chaleaux said. "A man who's been through what I have learns the value of kindness."

Hank's mother said, "I see."

"Those comments about that girl in the magazine, that little girl with her trussed-up bosoms, those were just an ancient male slang. I'm sorry if they offended you or disturbed your peace. A woman as beautiful as yourself deserves some peace. I hope you won't mind my saying this."

Hank expected his mother to react, either to blush or to get up and leave the compartment. But she had assumed a posture of stillness and made her face profoundly bored. It was the same look she wore when her suitors called, all these eager Larrys and Rons, with their real estate baritones, leaping into the buzz saw of her disregard.

"Anyway, it's getting late and I can see you'd like to rest." Chaleaux flicked off the light on the door of the compartment and sat again. The pattern on his trousers fluoresced slightly so that words appeared in the loose-hanging folds. NEVER. DARK.

To his surprise, Hank's mother said nothing.

"I only point to a picture like that because a boy of your son's age has certain thoughts, certain preoccupations. Pretending otherwise is no solution. It just creates delinquent pressures."

"I'm sure you know all about them," Hank's mother murmured.

"Not that Hank, a boy like Hank, would be involved in such things. It's only motives I'm speaking about. We all know what those would be, and there's nothing unnatural in them. Nothing at all. Even if he didn't think these thoughts during the day, they would come to him at night, when our weakness is revealed. He would think those thoughts that young men think. Who knows exactly what? The specific images and so forth. That's his business. I know what I'd be thinking about, Mom. With just the two of you in that house."

Hank's mother said, "Stop."

"You can't hide a child forever, can you? A boy's desires are perfectly natural. We all have desires." Chaleaux shook his head. "Even you've got some, Mom, underneath all those hairpins."

She issued a distressed sound and Hank said: "She wants you to shut up. Shut up."

"I know. I need to shut up. No harm in defending what

belongs to you, Hank. It's the right move. Nobody wants to see the woman he loves in a state of distress." Chaleaux licked his upper lip. "As for that conductor, he's not coming by again. He's supposed to. Says right in his rule book. But we're a good thirty miles out of Toledo and there's no more stops on this line. He's in that warm little break room, shooting the bull with the others. Or taking a nap, maybe. You could get up and try to find him, Mom, but I'm guessing you don't want to leave me alone with Hank. Your mind is full of bad outcomes. When you live in fear, fear becomes whatever you look at."

"Such a philosopher," Hank's mother said. Her jaw muscles bunched. "We didn't realize you were such a philosopher."

Chaleaux smiled and dipped his head, undoing her irony. "I'll tell you what your mom's really afraid of, Hank: she's scared to death that you'll try something heroic. She doesn't want her boy tangling with some loudmouth on a train. You could get hurt. But another part of her is afraid you'll do just fine, afraid of what that might mean. Because then, I think, it would be obvious what you deserved."

Hank sat clenching and unclenching his fists. He considered his options. He could fetch the conductor; that would mean leaving his mother alone with Chaleaux. He could attack the man, or at least shout at him. But these measures seemed absurd. Chaleaux wasn't really *doing* anything. He was just talking.

Outside, the night industries had fired up. Lights illuminated the squat shaft of the nuclear reactor that sat halfway between Sandusky and Toledo. A few years back, some kind of acid had gotten loose inside and eaten through six inches of steel, nearly causing a meltdown. It had been all over the news.

Chaleaux talked on, growing more relaxed. The movements of his throat were slow and elaborate; his eyes were hooded in shadow. "She's sort of trapped, Hank. You both are. Living in a town like Buffalo, taking the late train because it's the cheapest ticket and making sure you're the first ones on, so you can choose a place and protect it, the two of you, riding along with your shoulders brushing in the dark. She's trying to hold on to you, Hank. It's a certain kind of mentality."

Hank's mother said something under her breath, which Hank did not catch, and Chaleaux said, "I've heard all those words before, filled my mouth with their dumb heat. You're in the right, Mom. But you're not really mad at me. You're mad at that other one, the one who wronged you so long ago. How do you forgive a man like that, who won't stay put or do what he's told? And you—you're still a young woman. Vibrant. Alive. There are things you deserve. Not just money or comfort, but things in the way of flesh."

"If you so much as lift a hand—"

"No, no," Chaleaux said. He spoke now as if his words were plucked from a sad dream. "That's not what this is about. You know that. Violence does none of us any good. It's just a place we move towards or away from. There's nothing in it that lasts. Even Hank knows that. We have the same perspective, Hank and me. I look at him and I see a younger version of myself. You make that noise, Mom, as if you find that ridiculous. But we have more in common than you'd like to think. We have our thoughts about you, for instance, and we have the night and we have all the nights yet to come. Hank can't stay around forever, dressing and undressing in that room next to yours, taking showers, walking around in his tank top, both of you struggling to lift that unspeakable need onto the other. How do we undo need, Mom? Loosen its hold? I'm asking a question here, a serious question."

Nicholas Chaleaux looked at each of them, in turn, with an odd tenderness. He pulled out a cigarette from the coat on the seat beside him and put it between his lips. He flexed his arms and the muscles leaped into sharp relief. "He'll have to leave. You know that. It's just something men do to you. And once he's gone, he'll never come back. He'll visit. Bring you flowers and gifts and some bride for you to chew on. But he'll never really be back, like it was before, just the two of you."

Hank's mother was gazing out the window. The distant lights

of Toledo shone on her small face. She was still playing bored. Then she turned for just a second, a half second, and gazed at Hank imploringly and he felt the rough truth of it beneath his ribs.

"Now listen," Chaleaux said. "I need to smoke this cigarette, because I'm addicted to the damn things. This is one of *my* needs. And I know you don't like smoke all over your clothing and hair and skin, so I'm going to head down to the lounge. But before I do, I want to take another look at the two of you so I can save the image in my head. I'm sure I don't look like a man who would go in for that kind of thing. Your mom wouldn't give me that much credit, Hank. But it's not difficult to make a picture in my mind." Chaleaux closed his eyes and let the cigarette dangle from his lips as he spoke. "I can see the two of you on this train, in a darkened compartment, leaning into the heat of each other. Your mom's not looking out that window, Hank, not in this picture. She's looking at you—her sweet, handsome son. And I know what she's thinking, what her exact thoughts are, even if she never speaks them. It's a precious thing to witness: those certain moments of our lives we wish would never end."

Chaleaux opened his eyes, stood slowly, and, with a curious deference, folded his jacket over his arm. He opened the door to the compartment and slipped through.

Hank thought about how best to dismiss the man, with a curt comment, maybe, or a muttered curse. Or maybe he should apologize to his mother for failing to defend her honor more vigorously. He tried to envision himself comforting her.

She was staring out the window, at the snakes of smoke from the chimneys, the factories filled with sooty men.

"He was crazy, Mom. Drunk and crazy."

His mother only shook her head. She slumped in her seat. Her mouth hung open slightly; her eyes appeared unfocused. He wanted somehow to be able to restore the careful architecture of her self-assurance.

The train was slowing, pulling into the steel berth of the

Toledo station, where Hank's grandmother would meet them, enveloped by her shabby coat and smelling of rose water. For three days she would fret over them, in the yellow knotted warmth of the apartment she could no longer quite manage. And then she would hail them a taxi and hug them a bit too long and they would get back on the train and return home.

Hank stood and began to lift the luggage from the overhead rack. "We're here," he said. "We should get going. She'll be waiting."

His mother nodded and extended her hand, bent primly at the wrist. Hank felt her fingers on his palm. He lifted her to her feet and she weighed nothing at all. The skin around her mouth, which she moisturized each night with ardent little dabs of cream, had grown thin and papery. Pale slashes of scalp showed through where her hair was pulled tight. Her eyes were delicate cups of ink.

She buckled against Hank, and certain pictures flashed into his mind—of his mother at a different age—and his body tensed. She seemed to spring against this tension and her hands searched for a place on his body, settling on the small of his back. He wanted to pull away from her, the swallowing need. But she was holding him there and his body was responding and he knew then that Chaleaux was watching them from outside the compartment, that he had been watching all along.

"Don't grow up to be a man like that," she whispered. "Hank. Promise me."

His mother shuddered against him and his body replied with a fierce happy motion. She gasped a little. He thought about the arms of Nicholas Chaleaux: the thick veins and muscle, the crude lettering. His mother wanted to step back, but Hank held her—held her easily—and their bodies were together in the darkness. He bent down so that the soft hairs of his mustache brushed against her damp cheek and he squeezed her one final time and waited until her breath was shallow and urgent and hot on his ear before answering, "Yeah. I promise."

A JEW BERSERK
ON CHRISTMAS EVE

SUZANNE BLACET STEPPED BACK from the Blacet Christmas tree and let out a quiet trill. The tree was enormous, something like fifty feet tall. It stretched to the ceiling of the den, with its beveled wainscoting. "Traditions," Suzanne said. She paused for a moment and tilted her head, as if listening for a pleasing echo. "That's what we believe in here: traditions. Family traditions. Don't we, honey?"

"Yes, Maman," said Adrianna, called Dria, my girlfriend. We were in college, a couple of sweaty econ majors. We'd been together for eight months and four days. This was my first visit to the Blacet mansion, to meet her family, which meant that Dria was now, suddenly, against all dependable odds, willing to have sex with me. She was tucked beside me in an angora sweater that made me want to rub her chest with my cock until both of us burst into flames. Was this a tradition Maman could endorse? I sensed no.

Also in the room were Dria's father, Bud, and her little brother, Sandro. They were wearing identical Polo sweaters the color of Tang. Paco, the handyman, stood watch over the roaring fire. Madelina, the housekeeper, disbursed eggnog. She looked ready to murder everyone in the room.

Suzanne beckoned me to step forward, toward a large cedar box. Inside was a selection of bright silver tchotchkes. "Ornaments." Suzanne placed her hand on my forearm. "Relics of our past. We put them on the tree every year. As a way of remembering."

"That's great," I said.

"Choose one," Suzanne said. "This is the Blacet way." She pronounced her surname with a Parisian lilt (omitting the *t*) and laughed at her little rhyme.

"Really?" I said. "I mean, I don't want to take anyone's favorite."

Suzanne looked at her husband.

He was a short, thick man with the face of a grizzled cherub. "Nonsense!" Bud said. "Nonsense! Choose one! Go ahead!"

"Volume," Sandro said.

Bud fiddled with his hearing aid. He'd managed a steel forge before he married into Blacet money.

The ornaments looked priceless, all of them, little bells and angels and stars. I chose the shabbiest-looking one, some kind of pewter peg, and hung it on a low limb.

"Oh," Suzanne said. "Perfect. So perfect and shiny. Isn't that nice, Jacob?"

"Yes," I said. "Very pretty."

"Do you know what it is?"

"Not really," I said.

"It belonged to my Grandpere Marsen," she said. "His shoehorn."

"You were going to say butt plug, weren't you?" Dria whispered. "Weren't you, you dirty little Jew horn?"

JEW HORN. Was this a term I should have viewed as acceptable? No. But it was what Dria called me in her moods of amour, those brief, intense periods during which she wanted nothing more than to wriggle her soft little hand down the front of my good corduroys.

It was a horrible term, a slur, a clear indicator of Dria's various cultural pathologies. But I wanted to have sex with her *really badly*. I had certain ideas about what it would be like inside her, like the ocean, like flying, like licking marmalade off the good silver. I was not quite twenty years old.

Besides, dirty talk was a part of our routine. It was something Dria, so wealthy, so continental, so devoutly moisturized, required. She would get herself nice and loaded at a sorority party and call me "Jew horn" and "matzo fucker." And I, once I figured out the rules, called her "frog slut" and "Parisian whore." We'd call each other these things and press our bodies together, our naughty parts yearning for consummation and all the damp, chafing fabrics in between.

So much drunken hope! Isn't that a version of love also, some central, infant aspect of the thing: the dumb throb, the frantic seep? How else do we withstand the rest of the bullshit?

Anyway, I'm not going to go into how we met or how we broke up or the secret scars we acquired. That's part of some other, duller story. I'm going to stick to this one Christmas Eve, all the sweet damnation that came rushing at me, along with the nutmeg and smoke and old leather.

Dria had issued her promise. "You want to get that horn up there, don't you? All deep inside. It's going to be ready for you. But you have to wait until Christmas Eve. You have to be a patient little Hebrew."

❖   ❖   ❖

DINNER WAS A MASSIVE RACK OF LAMB, pale slabs of muscle spiced with Mrs. Dash and dressed in a neon mint jelly. The Blacets ate with grace and precision. I could never quite catch them chewing.

Suzanne addressed me through a maze of candelabras. "Tell us about your winter holiday. You celebrate Chanukah, I assume?"

"It's *Ha*nukkah," Sandro said. He spoke with the towering boredom of a fifteen-year-old; it pained him to correct the world's relentless ignorance.

"There are eight nights, and you light a candle for each. Why is that, Jacob?"

"Well," I said, "it commemorates the Maccabeans, who were a tribe of rebel fighters in antiquity. They were trying to liberate the Jews from the Romans, and at the same time, they were trying to keep the candles in the temple, the Old Temple, lit, which I believe was a commandment, one of God's, but they only had enough oil for one day, but the oil lasted for eight days. It was a miracle."

The Blacets looked at me, nakedly disappointed: this was what the Jews were putting up against the birth of the Savior?

"I think it's a terrific story, Joseph," Bud hollered.

"Jacob," Sandro said. "The guy's name is *Jacob*."

"Yes dear," Suzanne said.

"Which one was Jacob?" Bud said. "The one with the raincoat?"

"That's Joseph," Sandro said.

"Did he wind up in the hole?"

"You're thinking of Jeremiah, dear," Suzanne said. "The prophet."

"I thought Jeremiah was a bullfrog," Bud said.

Dria squealed out her pity laugh, then reached beneath the table and placed her hand on my belt buckle.

Dessert, a fruit gelée, was served by Madelina.

"Good meat, Mother," Bud said.

"Madelina made it," Sandro said.

Suzanne shot her son a look.

"Are we using the same butcher?" Bud said. "The old Kraut?"

"Don't say that, father," Dria said. "It's a slur. Kraut is a slur."

Suzanne looked at her husband. "Honestly, dear, Jacob doesn't want to hear about Germans."

Bud waved his hands in mock surrender.

"What does Hanukkah have to do with the twelve tribes?" Sandro wanted to know. He'd eaten fourteen slices of lamb and left his dessert untouched.

"I'm not sure, exactly," I said.

"Can you name them?" The little butterball leered at me. "Benjamin, Judah, Levi, Dan, that's the one that got lost—"

"Quit showing off," Dria said. "It's tacky. Everyone in this family is so tacky." She released my belt buckle and let her little hand drop down onto my crotch.

DRIA SENT ME OUT TO THE BACK PORCH with Bud. I assumed he would take this opportunity to determine whether I planned to deflower his daughter. (In fact Dria had lost her virginity a year earlier, to a Sigma Chi who had plied her with grain alcohol and Walt Whitman.) We stood in awkward silence, examining the acreage, the dark lip of night.

Suzanne was in the kitchen with Madelina. I had seen them huddled over the sink, enjoying the rich communion of disapproval.

Bud pulled a flask out, took a long slug, handed it to me.

I took a sip. "Wow."

"They get the real stuff," he screamed mysteriously. "From the viscount."

"It certainly tastes real."

"Goddamn Vichy money," Bud said, with unexpected rancor.

I took another swallow and stared at the dense stand of trees that bordered the property. Their trunks shone like pale fingers in the light from the house.

"Birch," Bud said sadly. He tapped his belly. "All right, let's get this show on the road. You ready, Jack?"

"Sir?"

Bud tucked the flask into the back pocket of his wool trousers. He trundled off the porch and toward a small shed, from which he removed two massive axes. He handed one to me. The idea was that, having drunk our bourbon, we would now chop wood. These activities struck me as best conducted separately, but I was in no position to object. This was the Blacet tradition, and I wanted more than anything to be obedient to this tradition, so that later, on the very eve of Christmas, I would be granted unlimited access to Dria's lovingly pruned lower half.

A large tree trunk had been placed, for our convenience, beneath the shed's motion-activated light. Bud spit into his palms. "You take that other end," he said.

My swings bounced off the wood in a manner that would soon result in the loss of one (or both) of my feet. Bud's blade bit into the wood, producing epic cracks. And then suddenly Paco was standing off to my left, like a grim apparition. He looked at me with something that didn't quite rise to the level of reproach and took the ax from my blistered hands.

They went at the wood with a frantic devotion. These were full-bodied strokes of the sort I associated with Paul Bunyan. Their cheeks marbled with exertion, the rapture of hard labor. They moved from the ends of the log toward the center, until they were touching at the flanks, their puffs and grunts fallen into a steady rhythm.

LATER, DRIA AND I FOUND OUR WAY into the larder. We ground pelvic bones and discussed sleeping arrangements. They had stashed me in the basement, while Dria was on the third floor, next to the master bedroom.

"It'll be a secret mission," she said. "You'll have to be cunning, like Odysseus."

"But your parents."

"Wait until after midnight. They sleep like the dead." She

looked up at me with her chin flashing. "I'll be ready for you, Jay." She lifted her skirt and showed me the long white thighs. Her tongue was hot with eggnog.

Then we heard footsteps and jumped away from each other just as Madelina opened the door. She was in a silent ecstasy, pretending to be surprised, pretending not to understand the scene before her.

"We were checking something," Dria said.

"Is that so?"

"Yes, it is."

"What were you *sh*ecking, Dria?" Madelina said, in her merciless accent. "Were you shecking if we had beef bouillon? Or maybe you were shecking if we had saltines. And you needed someone to help, a tall someone to see on those high shelves? But of course that is none of my business."

"That's right," Dria said sharply. "There are some things that are nobody's business. You of all people should know that."

The two of them exchanged a look of accumulated recrimination.

"Your mother is in the parlor," Madelina said slowly.

We made our way back and listened to Suzanne Blacet as she detailed the legacy of her forebears, who had served in the court of Louis Quatorze, Napoléon's army, the Académie des sciences. Dria had mentioned none of this. It was unnecessary. Her very manner, the grace wafting from her gestures, announced her lineage.

I felt as if I were in the midst of many confusing secrets. It hadn't occurred to me that this was the central purpose of family: the production of secrets, the elaborate concealment of embarrassing truths. I still thought of my family in childish terms, as a lovable inconvenience.

Suzanne talked on and on. The fire snapped. Dria sat listening to her maman and licking her lips.

❖   ❖   ❖

I'D DRUNK TOO MUCH EGGNOG—that much was clear. There was also the wine at dinner, and the bourbon. I was not much of a drinker even under the best of circumstances. But my nerves, my wanting to do things right, had gotten the best of me.

Thus: my bed was spinning. I got up and sat on the toilet and put my head between my legs. It wasn't entirely clear to me how I was supposed to get to Dria's room. At midnight, I stumbled up the stairs to the first floor. All the lights were off, but the endless candelabras twinkled in the moonlight and their beauty held me for a few moments.

Then a strange smell washed over me, a musk of some kind, which seemed to be emanating from the rear bathroom, where I had gone to collect myself after Madelina caught us necking. I thought perhaps it was Madelina herself, taking a perfumed bath. There is no reason, aside from dumb animal curiosity, that I should have tiptoed toward that door. Then again, at that particular moment, at most of the important human moments, dumb animal curiosity is pretty much the ball game.

The door was ajar, of course, and aromatic steam puffed out. I recognized the scent: eucalyptus. I should mention that this bathroom was—like all the Blacet bathrooms—tremendous and ornately mirrored, a style no doubt inspired by the palatial shitters of the Sun King.

I peeked inside. The mirror was mostly fogged over, but it allowed me a view of what I had thought was a bathtub. In fact it was a shower and steam room with a small tile bench, where Bud and Paco sat together. They were both quite naked, Bud red with the heat, Paco a luminous umber.

This was strange enough to disorient me a little. Then Paco began scrubbing Bud's shoulders with a pumice stone. Bud's eyelids drooped with pleasure, like a dog having his ears scratched. He lowered his forehead onto Paco's sturdy shoulder.

I wasn't sure what to think. There was some part of me that figured this was simply how the wealthy did things—their longtime servants performed such duties. And then there was another part of me that could see, simply by the relaxed posture of their bodies, that this was something more than a professional arrangement, a prelude to further ministrations.

I shut the door; my heart was chopping.

I should have gone back downstairs at this point. But I had my own needs. Dria was waiting, with her eager downy loins. She was ready and my body knew what ready meant and I made for the stairs.

THE SECOND FLOOR WAS PITCH-BLACK. I crept across the thick carpets and waited for my eyes to adjust. I could feel someone else in the room and spun around to find a noblewoman, painted in somber colors, glowering down at me from a gilded frame. In one hand she held a black squirrel, in the other a small brown nut.

I hurried toward a door I hoped would lead to the stairs. But this was the main kitchen, with a vast counter, upon which the remains of our dinner lay congealing. Then I heard a voice and ducked down, behind a wall of pans.

"Who's there?" Madelina said. "Is there someone there? Madame?"

A second voice—faint, nakedly frightened—said, "Is someone there, tía?"

"Silence," Madelina whispered. Her footsteps carried her past the counter. She latched the swinging door shut. I could see a dark hem and the plump calves beneath. With a grunt she lifted something from the counter. "Now," she said. "Turn around. All the way. Do it, little lamb. Do it, or you won't get any. Hold still. Hold still, little lamb."

The only sound during all this was a moist stroking I couldn't place. Skin was touching skin, but it sounded medicinal, not sexual. Madelina finished whatever she was doing and I heard her approach the counter. The next sound was unmistakable: a brisk metallic hiss. She was sharpening a knife.

I didn't know what to do. Perhaps I was dreaming—this was all an odd, pickled dream. The sharpening stopped and Madelina rasped, "Who's there? Who is that I hear?"

I froze. What would I do if she came any closer? Could I successfully flee? No, my socks would slip on the wood floor and loyal Madelina would set upon me with her knife and carve snow angels into my thorax. I was an intruder, after all, a Jew who had groped the princess in the pantry. The family would close ranks. I had drunk too much liquor and gone berserk, after Adrianna refused to blow my Jew horn. Madelina was speaking again. "Who's there? Is that a little lamb? A greedy little lamb?" She had turned away from the counter and was moving toward the far end of the kitchen.

Then I heard another weird noise, a kind of snuffling whimper.

I inched my head above the counter. Madelina was dressed in a long, dark robe, a sort of nun's habit. She knelt before a small alcove, into which was wedged a large glistening doll. Then the doll whimpered again and I could see that the doll was Sandro, that he had folded himself into this small space, which was in fact the dumbwaiter. His skin appeared to have been slathered in some kind of lotion. There was a bowl to Madelina's left, half full of what my mother would have called drippings—the liquid fat gathered from the broiler beneath the lamb.

With her left hand, Madelina stabbed at the platter beside her and slowly raised a slice of lamb toward Sandro's mouth. She was speaking softly now. "Mi gordito," she said. "Tienes hambre, eh?"

It was entirely unclear to me how Sandro had fitted himself inside the dumbwaiter. He was, as I've mentioned, a fat child, folded upon himself; his limbs were pinned against his flanks. His mouth struggled for the meat. Madelina flicked his forehead to still him. She held the slice beneath his nose, drew it away, dragged it across his forehead, across the bridge of his nose.

Sandro's eyes began to tear up.

"Don't cry, gordito. The Lord provides. Do you believe that, little lamb?"

Sandro nodded.

She continued to drag the meat across his face, like a sick rag. "But you must suffer for your sins on this night, yes?"

At last she let him bite down on one end. The other end she placed in her own mouth. They chewed until their lips were touching. This wasn't kissing, but something more tender and religious.

I wish I could report that I proceeded directly out of that house, to the nearest police station. But no. I was still drunk, and now quite frightened. I couldn't imagine heading back down to the basement. I had to see Dria, not to make love to her, nothing that complicated. I simply needed to cower under her covers until daylight. I was certain she was innocent of all this.

THERE WAS A LONG HALLWAY on the third floor, with wheezing radiators and many doors on either side. Dria had told me she was in the room at the end of the hall. But was I meant to turn left or right at the top of the stairs? The prospect of a wrong decision paralyzed me. What would I find behind the mystery door: Mrs. Blacet copulating with a baboon?

So I guessed left and staggered that way. I thought about my own family, gathered down in Baltimore—the neurotic, self-critical, petty lot of them—cheating at Scrabble and complaining about acid reflux. I saw my uncle Morris smuggling a *Nation* into the bathroom, a look of assumed failure etched on his brow. My cousin Roy would be spitting at the girl cousins on the stoop. Never had these common miseries seemed so alluring.

Here was the door, big and funereal like all the Blacet doors. I thought of Madelina down below, auditioning for the Inquisition, and pushed the thing open. The familiar scent of Dria was upon me: lavender and new stockings. The expanse of her childhood habitat unfurled before me, pink and ruffled, and I felt marginally safer.

"You made it," she whispered.

"Yeah," I said. "Listen . . ."

But I couldn't complete my thought. She was sitting up in bed, naked to the waist, her small breasts beaming at me. I was overcome by gratitude, by relief.

"Get over here," she said. "I've been waiting. I'm *ready*. Were you cunning? You were, weren't you? Long johns! You're so cute. Get *over* here." She pulled me into an embrace. "You're trembling. Are you cold?"

My head shook itself. "I'm a little, I guess, freaked out."

Dria looked at me with her distinguished nose, her lioness eyes. "That is so *sweet*," she said. "Don't be freaked out, Jay. This is going to be amazing. You were so good. You waited so patiently. Look what I have for you!" She gestured toward her chest. "These are for you!" She placed my hands on them. "Come onto the bed."

Then I was on the bed and Dria was yanking at my waistband.

I said, "I'd like to—could we talk?"

"You're nervous, aren't you?"

Dria lifted the covers. I could feel the warmth of her lower body as a wave. It made me want to crawl down there and curl up with my cheek on her mons pubis. That seemed a first step. But Dria had her own agenda. She, too, had been waiting. She, too, was not quite twenty years old. Her body was a configuration of inept desires loosely knit into action. She my took my hand and showed me her readiness. She tossed my long johns away.

"I saw some weird stuff," I managed. "Downstairs."

"You're still drunk, aren't you? You're so cute when you're drunk!" She reached for me. "He's not drunk, though. He's standing straight up. He's ready, isn't he?"

I admitted that he was ready.

"That means we're both ready."

Dria was in one of her states, the rush of the thing, the anxiety, making her grabby. I was supposed to get on top of her. Those were her orders. I was supposed to open her legs and place my young readiness against hers and get the party started. And I might actually have done so; my body was poised to enact its ecstatic will—except that I heard a noise.

"What the hell was that?" I said.

"Nothing."

Then it came again, a muffled sneeze.

"Nothing," Dria said again.

The closet swung open and there was Suzanne Blacet, in a fancy sleeping gown, her hair gathered into a chignon.

I tried to roll off Dria, but she held me fast. "*Maman!*" she snarled. Her tone was not one of shock, or fear, but rage.

They began to speak very quickly.

"I'm sorry," Suzanne said.

"I knew you'd find some way to announce yourself!"

"Surely you don't think—"

"I do!"

"There were dust mites, dear."

"You could have used the peephole!"

"This is my *home.*"

"You've scared him," Dria said. "You've scared Jacob. Now he's going to be all freaked out. You're freaked out now, aren't you Jacob?"

"Yes," I said, and reached to cover my nakedness with the duvet.

"*See,*" Dria shrieked. Her voice was zooming toward a weepy timbre.

Suzanne took a step toward the bed. "Do you honestly think I'd want your friend to see me in this state?" Her bare face showed a rumpled beauty.

"This is a misunderstanding," I said. "I came to tuck your

daughter in. I meant no disrespect. I was just heading downstairs, to my room."

"Nonsense," Dria said. "You're not going anywhere. I was ready. I'm *ready*." She was crying now.

"Calm down," Suzanne said. "You are such a little actress. Jacob is not an unintelligent boy. Don't underestimate him."

"You're ruining this!"

"I'm not ruining anything, Adrianna. Don't be silly. Don't make this a *scene*. Listen, Jacob," she said, in a measured tone. She smoothed her robe and seated herself delicately on the ottoman beside the bed. "I spoke to you earlier about traditions. We are a family with traditions. In the old days—I am talking about several generations ago, in France—most of the marriages were arranged. Girls of a certain standing were betrothed to noblemen, much older men usually. The occasion of the wedding night was a rather perilous situation. Do you understand? There was a dowry at issue. These girls were quite innocent. And some of these gentlemen—their behavior was somewhat less than honorable. The result was that families insisted the mother of the bride, or a suitable proxy, be allowed to witness the inaugural coupling. There was nothing prurient in this. It was merely an effort to safeguard the experience, which can be so formative."

I glanced down at Dria, sprawled beneath me, aghast. "Oh God," she said. "You're making us sound medieval!"

"I am explaining the situation," Suzanne said calmly. "This tradition is not limited to our family. It is a widespread and sensible practice. Dria communicates with me about her life, as she will wish her children to communicate with her. She has chosen you. I accept that. I have not asked her to take a vow of chastity until marriage. I have allowed her the freedom to do as she wishes. We are a modern family, Jacob. But she is my only daughter."

"We're not married," Dria said miserably. "This isn't our wedding night."

"Nor do I expect you to get married. You are young."

"He's going to think I'm all crazy."

"Nonsense," Suzanne said. "He will think that you are loyal to your family, which is not yet a sin. I have asked that Adrianna, as a member of our family, uphold our traditions. I intend this as no aspersion. You strike me as a perfectly nice young man. I admire your religion. The Jews are an industrious peoples."

"Just get out, Maman! Go back to your room!"

Suzanne shook her head. "Do not raise your voice to me in my own home," she said, then turned back to me. "We are an open family, Jacob. We have no secrets. But we do have a saying, from the French: 'What the moon may know, the sun need not.' Isn't that a lovely sentiment? It has brought us much happiness. I would advise you not to become too concerned with the customs or morals of others. You'll have a very long, dull journey if you do. There is my daughter. She has waited a long time to make love to you—"

"*Maman*—"

"—and you have waited, too. I will remain in the hall for two minutes. If you wish to return to your room, Jacob, you may do so."

Suzanne left the room and Dria looked at me. It was clear her mother held this power over her. She was red with the shame.

"It's okay," I said.

"I was so *ready*." Dria sighed. "Now you think I'm crazy." She was lying naked under the eiderdown, her warm chest hiccuping with disappointment. I stroked her along the hip.

"You should go," she said. "I know you want to go." She reached up to touch my cheek. "I did want that filthy Jew horn inside me," she said, nostalgically.

THE MECHANISMS OF DESIRE are so strange in our species, residing half in our madness, half in our hearts. Who can say what gestures will light the wick? It must be easier for the rest of the animals, a matter of the glands.

Or maybe it was this easy for me, as I lay next to Adrianna

Blacet on Christmas Eve. Her glands told her to start breathing more deeply. Her glands told her to drag her fingertips down my chest. My glands, in turn, became suddenly attuned to her, stark naked at last. How long my glands had waited for this, eight months of swollen prelude.

There was so much perversity blooming in that house, Bud and Paco nestled in their man lodge, Sandro greased and whimpering, Suzanne ready to witness our fumbling coitus. These were disturbing facts. I agreed. *I agreed.* But I couldn't do anything about them, really. At best, I could run off into the world of the allegedly normal with a scandalous story to tell. The world has enough of those.

Consider this one: a teenage girl announces she's been impregnated by God and gives birth to his bastard son in a donkey barn. Strange stuff. Whereas Dria—she wasn't strange at all. She wasn't angry at her mother, either. Not really. She wanted, instead, a grand occasion for hope. Our bodies yearned for contact. Her lips searched for mine.

We did hear the door click behind us, just as I slipped inside Dria. She let out a purr of surprise, which registered as a soft vibration. But we were alone in the cave of our desire, as true lovers always are.

By morning, there was a fresh coat of snow on the ground. Madelina set out a breakfast to feed the Huns. The fire was already blazing. We gathered in the den, drowsy and grateful, our doubles lives neatly tucked beneath the tree, with the gifts.

"Did anyone hear Santa last night?" Bud said.

Dria, seated primly beside me, rolled her eyes. "He asks this every year."

Suzanne looked at Sandro.

"I didn't hear a thing," he said sulkily.

"That Santa," Bud said. He turned and flashed me an almost imperceptible wink. "He's one quiet son of a bitch."

AKEDAH

YOU ARE THE MOTHER OF A SOLDIER returned from war. He is all
you have. Your husband is dead. He married you young, moved
you across the state to Philadelphia, away from your family and
your congregation. Then he died in a trolley accident. And now
your son, Ike, is home from the war, from the Battle of the Bulge,
from the coast of France, which you imagine as someplace white
and jagged, but he smells different now, of cigarettes and rank
cotton. It bothers you especially because you work in a laundry.
Your hands are perpetually chapped; the hot water stings.

Ike does day labor and spends weekends on the front stoop. He
doesn't talk to the hoodlums, but he doesn't talk to you, either.

Then he disappears. It's like smoke the way he goes. You buy pets, a turtle, a cat, to keep him company while you're away at work. He watches them for a few days, then they're gone, too. You cook for him, the old favorites, recipes from your grandmother. He eats bread with hunks of butter. After supper he slips out the back door and returns in a strange hat, cuts on his knuckles. One day your neighbor Mrs. Stochansky, another widow, a big mouth, informs you that Ike has been arrested. When he comes home, you ask him if it's true. His smile is a wince. You touch his shoulder and the muscles turn to stone.

You take the trolley to the shul, to consult the rabbi, an old man with a delicate veil of wrinkles around his eyes. You explain the situation, taking care not to burnish your account. He nods slowly. The boy is lost, he says. You must be patient.

You want to ask: *How patient?* But before you can say anything, another word, he spits into his palm and says, The Lord is patient.

One night, you return home late from work and hear a shrieking, something animal, coming from his room. You think: a girl. You think: what has he done? The noise stops, then starts again. You call his name. You walk quietly to his door and pause, breathing hard. A memory comes to you from childhood, of walking in the woods behind your father, his broad back surging forward, dark fringes of shadow, the struggle to keep up. Where was he taking you?

Isaac, you whisper. Darling, what is it?

You ease the door open and he is sitting on his bed staring at you, as if he has been waiting for this moment his entire life.

Isaac. Darling.

The noise comes out of him.

You close the door.

A week later he vanishes. You call the police, visit the hospitals. Nobody knows a thing about your boy. Then word arrives: he has been found near Allentown. He has hurt two men and, apparently, a woman. Something outside a bar. No weapon found. For his own protection he has been placed in an asylum.

Every other Sunday, you visit. They keep your son on a safe ward. Everything padded. From beneath his tangled hair the eyes of your father stare out at you.

Nothing wrong with me, he says. It was a misunderstanding. Ma, he says.

When his hands tremble, he says, Crap coffee in this dump.

At home you read all the hopeful magazines. You cut out the new recipes and make them with great care: Chicken with 40 Cloves of Garlic, the Perfect Tuna Casserole, Twice-Broiled Cod. You look at these beautiful dishes on your kitchen table. There's no way to save them, so you throw them away.

In *Modern Marvels* you read about Dr. James Dybek. He is a great surgeon whose procedure calms the mentally disturbed. It is so safe, so humane, that patients often sing during the operation. There is a photo of a young man smiling. His mother tells the reporter, "We live in a country of miracles."

There is no information about how to contact Dybek, but adversity is the mother of invention and you are the mother of a boy in trouble. You contact an editor at the magazine, a doctor at his institution, a cantor for whom you have done some volunteer work. You send letters. These people treat you with a stifling deference. You have become a person in crisis: single-minded, without embarrassment.

You don't pray. Then you do. Then you don't. One day a telegram arrives and confirms an appointment for your son, Isaac _____, on the twenty-second day of the first month at twelve noon. The hospital is in Pittsburgh. A secretary has signed on behalf of the doctor.

The day arrives and Ike looks different when you come to pick him up. Relaxed, you think. The doctor wants to send an orderly along, just in case, but you insist that won't be necessary. You and your son travel alone, on a bus, on the brand-new turnpike.

He sleeps most of the way, his legs tensing like when he was a boy.

You pass through Conshohocken, Lebanon, through maples and ash, balsam fir, wild sassafras, you pass into the Great Valley with its dogwood and dotted hawthorn, into the Dutch lowlands, whorls of barley. In Blue Mountain, the bus stops for gas and the passengers pile out to use the bathroom and sip stale coffee. Ike insists on carrying the bags you've packed, full of sandwiches and underwear. He has not asked you where you are taking him, or why.

In the restroom, you gaze into the mirror. Your hair is pulled back into a knot. The flesh at the base of your neck is loose. Your eyes are red with complicity. You look 137 years old.

When you walk outside, Ike is slumped against the rear bumper of the bus. They have given him pills at the hospital. You see this now.

The bus passes through Somerset, up the Allegheny Plateau; the tips of the Appalachians become visible, glowing absurdly in the west. Then the Three Rivers come into view and there are white birds on the banks and your son opens his eyes and sees them and for the briefest moment his arms rise. A flutter, a chance, the wonder of flight.

At the hospital, you are directed to a waiting room. There is a bustle of nurses, a clean floor, the bloom of iodine. Your son says nothing. He is used to hospitals. A pretty nurse leads him away to be prepped for the procedure.

You see him next as you enter the operating room. The same nurse is walking him to the long table. His smock barely covers his nakedness. His arms and legs have softened, grown thicker. He is twenty-seven years old, strong as a bull. You can see, from his gait, that the sedatives have worn off. But he climbs onto the table and lies down and his movements are docile.

The famous doctor hurries into the room. He is short and bald. He has a sharp white beard, thick spectacles. He ties on his mask and nods briskly at the nurses. Your son is beneath him. There are assistants all around now, a photographer with a flash camera. Behind the doctor stands a man holding a box covered in linen. Someone murmurs in your ear, You may watch if you wish, ma'am. But we do not recommend it.

You want to hold your son's hand. You approach the table. His hair has been shorn. There are black marks on his skull, on his eyelids. An assistant is explaining what will happen, choosing his words kindly. You can't concentrate.

That memory flashes again, of your father leading you into the woods. But your father is dead. Your husband is dead. It is only you and your son, who will not ask where you have taken him, who is being bound upon the table, which has become an altar, and his hand is there for you, so you step forward and hold on. Then a voice is speaking to you: *Lay not your hand upon the child, neither do you any thing unto him: for now I know that you fear God.*

You say, Yes, I do fear God. You say this loud enough to stop the bustle of nurses and one begins speaking to you in urgent, soothing tones. The great doctor himself looks disturbed. Behind him is the man holding the box, which has fallen open a little. You can see the glint of the instruments.

Please, you say. There has been a mistake. I've made a mistake.

Your son lies perfectly still, his skull aglow. You will not let go of his hand, but he has let go of yours. He looks at you calmly.

Don't you think I trust you, Ma?

The doctor addresses you from across the table. Listen to me, my good woman. I will save this young man. Then he nods, almost imperceptibly, and you feel your body rising, being pulled away from his body and toward the door and you look back one final time and your son smiles at you before the blade burrows in.

Afterward, there is nothing in those eyes, no fear, no desire. He becomes invisible. Or, rather, he becomes a memory, a cloud through which you must walk toward your own death. You see him as a little boy, flapping his wings at the white birds along the Delaware shore. You see him in the darkness of that bus, waking to the gulls above the Allegheny. You see this and your heart buzzes three times. Then a jolt. You were his mother. He was an angel. How did you miss that?

HAGAR'S SONS

COHEN (AT WORK)

The call startled him. Cohen rarely received calls at work. The voice—silky, vaguely hostile—belonged to Mr. Vanderweghe's assistant.

"Mr. Vanderweghe will need to see you," she said.

"Of course," Cohen said. "I'll just, let me look—" He glanced at his desk calendar. It was blank, aside from a note in the lower right-hand corner, which read *diapers, rubylicious (huggies): Remember!*

"Now, Mr. Cohen."

Cohen wanted to ask whether he should bring the preliminary

results from his currency project, but the line went dead. He carefully redacted the Huggies note and hurried to the bathroom to brush his teeth.

MISSION

Vanderweghe was dressed in the dark wool of a minor Dickens villain; the suit collar bit into his jowls. Cohen had seen him only once before, on the day of his arrival.

"Cohen."

"Sir."

Vanderweghe nodded for him to sit.

"The sheik has asked to meet with you."

Cohen nodded reflexively. He had never heard of any sheik and, in fact, knew next to nothing about the firm for which he worked. Four months ago, he had been plucked from the research division at Salomon Smith Barney at the behest of someone, he assumed, much more powerful than himself, and installed in a small office and told to study yen mode differentials until further notice. He was happy to have escaped Wall Street, the vulgar, caffeinated masculinity of the place, the bellowing traders with their sirloin tongues. Cohen had a high-strung wife, a colicky newborn, significant debt. He did not, as such, sleep.

"The sheik is a valued client, as you know."

"Of course," Cohen said.

"*Valued.*"

There was a pause. "What might the sheik want with me?"

"If I knew that—" Vanderweghe's face twisted into an abrupt silence. "Get your suit pressed," he murmured, and handed Cohen a file. Inside was a glossary of Arabic terms, cultural customs, and a history of the New Emirate. The only itinerary was a handwritten note informing him that he would be picked up at eight the next morning.

❖   ❖   ❖

"I don't unnerstand," Chantal said. "They say you go, you just go? No plane ticket? No return date? It's the year 2000, not medieval times. You are not a slave on a galley ship."

Chantal was the Wife. She was French Tunisian. Fine bones. Black hair. A quick temper that blotched her cheeks.

"It's my job," Cohen said.

"Your job!" Chantal dug her spoon into a pint of gelato.

The baby was wailing.

Cohen had met Chantal at a Salomon Brothers function. They had gotten drunk and done what young couples do. A few weeks later she was pregnant and Cohen, wanting to do right, married her. His father was dead, his mother was thrilled. His younger sister, floating somewhere outside Santa Cruz in an irritable lesbian phase, said, "Do yourself a favor and get a paternity test."

Now they lived in a one-bedroom in Queens. Chantal was an aspiring model, but the pregnancy had ruined her skin. She blamed Cohen. Ruby was a pork chop, a doll face, she maybe had his mouth, he thought so, and a little Mohawk, but she cried so much.

Cohen unstrapped her from the high chair and stared at her face. It was rutted with distress, a red pecan. "What's the matter, baby?" Cohen said. "It's okay, baby."

Chantal made a fart noise with her cheek. "That's right. Reason with the baby. And what if you never come back? You go to this Arab place with your Jew name and your nose—"

"He's a major client. This is an *honor*." He rubbed Ruby's back and felt her begin to subside. "It could lead to things."

"And if you never come back?"

Cohen sighed. His apartment smelled of baby shit and artificial lavender. All the lamps were broken. "Stop being dramatic."

Chantal thwacked her spoon against the wall. The baby tensed. He felt her engine knock, then catch—the inexorable ascent to a tantrum.

"Americans! So naive. So sure of yourselfs. Did you get the fucking uggies? The *uggies*! I thought no."

TRIP OVER

The plane looked like an shark, long and sleek. It was unmarked beyond the call letters, and Cohen was the only passenger on it. A pair of young women served him shirred eggs and dispatched him to a couchette, where he fell into a profound sleep. He woke over a blue expanse decorated with islands in the shape of Arabic characters. These were the Suras, the Emirate's latest project, 114 luxury islands.

"All dredged from the Gulf," one of the beauties explained. "That one is the Thunder. The Moon is there. The Spoils of War. Oh, and that one is Repentance. Repentance is new!"

The articulation of the letters was astounding, but Cohen wondered aloud who, aside from plane passengers fluent in Arabic, would be able to appreciate the project.

"God will see them," the girl said softly, "and smile."

WHAT COHEN NOTICED

1. Everything was clean.

Immaculate. It was as if a giant vacuum had sucked up all unwanted matter and left behind fresh carnations. This was moving to Cohen, whose floors at home were scattered with half-chewed mini-waffles, who was himself sheathed in a thin, chemically detectable layer of poop. He soaked in the tub for an hour.

2. It was like being in a casino.

There were no clocks anywhere. The surfaces sparkled. The air was richly oxygenated. Cohen was staying on the top floor of the Haj. From his window he counted 143 cranes. There were hotels in the shapes of a crescent, a scimitar, an oyster shell. Directly across from him a row of workers sat in slings half a mile above the earth, squeegeeing the windows of a building whose summit Cohen could not see.

3. The Emirate was exploding.

This is what his tour guide said, over and over. He pronounced the word "ixploding." The new civic projects included an underground aviary with more than eighteen thousand species of birds, a library of antiquated books larger than Alexandria's, a facsimile of the Temple Mount rendered in electrum. His guide had a fascist's passion for statistics and the feline smile of a pharaoh. Did Cohen know how many tons of marble had been quarried to create the Jubilation Pavilion?

Cohen called home three times. Chantal refused to answer.

BLADE NIGHT

He dreamed of his father, hunched in his recliner, lecturing the world on its failings. His father who had flunked out of college and fought in the Korean War, then flunked out of college again and sold insurance to widows. Death: his first and only ally. That was the joke.

"Dad?" Cohen said.

His father made no indication of having heard him.

The baby started wailing.

"That's Ruby," Cohen said. "That's your granddaughter."

His father drew a knife from his coat pocket and calmly punched it into his own stomach. Cohen woke with his ribs pounding. It took him a full minute to remember where he was.

HIGH ABOVE THE EARTH, AN OMELET

In the morning, a butler led Cohen to a private elevator, which opened onto a helipad atop his hotel. He was whizzed to a second helipad and driven along a narrow path to an egg-shaped platform whose means of suspension was unclear. At the center of the platform a table set for two awaited. The sheik wore a crisp dishdasha and sunglasses. To his left, a chef stood at attention behind an omelet station.

"Mr. Cohen," the sheik said.

"Good morning," Cohen said. He wasn't sure whether he should shake hands or bow.

The sheik made a sweeping gesture. The breeze rippled his headdress. The distant cranes were toys. Cohen suffered a wave of vertigo.

"You like eating outside? The prophets felt the same way. They did their best thinking on mountains." The sheik was younger than Cohen had expected. His accent sounded Southern Californian. "Everything good so far?"

"Very nice," Cohen said. "Spectacular." Some miles away, the glittering girdle of the Emirate gave way to a drab yellow.

"You know how much that suite runs? Eleven thou a night. Seriously, right? No worries." He lifted his glasses and rubbed his eyes, then let them drop back into place. A Bloody Mary appeared in his hand. "Agassi and Sampras played tennis right where we're sitting. You seen either of those guys play?" The sheik drained his Bloody Mary. "What sort of omelet you want? This man here, Bernard, makes the finest omelet on the planet. He's Belgian. Flemish. Name an ingredient. Any ingredient." The sheik waited for him.

"Tomatoes?" Cohen said. "Goat cheese?"

"Come *on*," the sheik said. He ordered shaved black truffle and foie gras.

The sheik began to discuss an actress he admired. She had starred in a cable television program about female astronauts. He had flown her over for a special screening sponsored by the Ministry of Culture. A parade had been held. The sheik wanted it known that he had not slept with this actress, despite the opportunity. Their relationship was professional. The Emirate would soon initiate a space program.

The omelets arrived. They were impeccable, diaphanous, the sort of omelets that deserved their own television show.

The sheik picked up a knife. "So you wanna know why you're here."

"It has been a little mysterious," Cohen said.

"Yeah, Arab customs. Here's the deal: the sheik needs your advice."

"The sheik? I thought—aren't you the sheik?"

The man across from him laughed. "No, man. I'm his nephew."

Cohen knocked his forehead with the heel of his palm and laughed and took a huge, relieved bite of omelet. "Of course I'll offer advice. That's what we, the firm, get paid—"

"The sheik asks this of *you*, Mr. Cohen." The nephew removed his sunglasses and narrowed his red eyes. "You understand?"

"Not really," Cohen said.

The nephew smiled without much warmth. He produced an envelope, upon which Cohen's full name was embossed in gold. "It's all good," he said.

WHO ARE YOU?

Inside was an invitation to the royal track. Cohen didn't know what to do. It was Saturday, the office was closed. He called home.

Chantal answered on the first ring. "Dan'el! Is it you? Where have you been?"

"Here," he said. "I'm here."

"Why you don't call? I thought something terrible—"

"I *did* call," Cohen said. "Three times. The machine didn't pick up."

"The fucking machine!" Chantal cursed in French. "You know how I hate the fucking machine!"

"Calm down," Cohen said.

"You travel to this place, like you're some kind of James Bonds."

"It's a business trip," Cohen said.

"So why there's no number to call? Which kind of business is that?"

Cohen moved the receiver away from his ear and waited. Chantal's mother had been an aspiring opera singer. She appeared at their wedding, unannounced, drunk, with a man younger than Cohen and too much rouge. Chantal wore hers the same way, glamorously bruised. Cohen told her she didn't need that stuff, she was beautiful, never mind the pimples. The makeup made him nervous to touch her face when they made love, which wasn't a lot these days but it did happen. It was something they could still give each other. Cohen wanted to be able to touch her face, to undo some of the worry there. She was stuck; they both were. He closed his eyes and felt a stab of pity, the unpleasant sensation of love draining from his sympathies.

"How's Ruby?" he said.

Chantal yelled something in French. She began to cry. Then Ruby began to cry.

"Let me talk to her," Cohen said. "Let me say hello to the baby."

The line went dead.

SHIPS OF THE DESERT

The royal track was a dirt strip flanked by highways. Cohen sat beside the sheik's nephew in a canary-yellow Hummer and gazed at the far end of the strip. The winner's circle, a patch of lawn, glowed against the sand.

"Kentucky blue," the nephew whispered to Cohen. His breath smelled of limoncello. "The real shit. They flew these guys in from Louisville, sod specialists. Like five of them, all named Bob. They thought they were going to stay in tents."

Cohen wanted to ask the sheik's nephew what his name was, but events seemed to have progressed beyond that point. "Is the sheik here?" he said.

"Somewhere."

A metallic siren sounded above them. The nephew pointed

to a small corrugated compound. A procession of camels lumbered forth, each with a tiny rider in colorful silks.

"They look like kids," Cohen said.

"They are! Pakistanis, a few from Sudan. The Pakis are stronger with the whip." The nephew bellowed across the track at a young sheik, who grabbed his crotch and spit over his shoulder. They both laughed. "Fucking Al Fayeed."

"The jockeys are really kids?" Cohen said.

"Yeah, we buy them from their parents." The nephew shook his head and giggled. "Come on, man. Don't be so gullible."

The windows of the Hummer scrolled down and the heat socked Cohen in the face. A bell sounded. The camels took off. The caravan of SUVs lurched after them. None of the drivers were watching the other drivers, because they were watching the camels and yelling into walkie-talkies and smoking.

The nephew was rammed from behind. He laughed and snatched an energy drink from a refrigerated tank built into the dashboard. "Ships of the fucking desert, man. I just made forty-five thousand dollars. Nice fucking work."

Cohen asked if he might visit the clubhouse.

"You're gonna miss the second race. There's only three. You got to drop a deuce or what?"

WHIRLIGIG

Inside the cinder block clubhouse were a bartender and an old man nibbling at an ice-cream bar. Cohen asked the bartender for a soda water and got tonic instead.

The trip had been a mistake. He was not someone who did well in unstable situations. His father had told him this long ago, at an amusement park, after he threw up on the whirligig. "So rides aren't for you. So stay off them." The tonic was flat.

Cohen closed his eyes and saw Ruby on her changing table, the puddles of rosy fat. He wanted to take a bite out of her thigh, just a little one, but she was busy weeping. And then Cohen himself was choked up, thinking about how much he loved her and how perhaps useless his love was.

Outside, the race bell sounded.

"Beware the prerogatives of wealth."

Cohen looked up.

The old man smiled at him. He looked like an Arab Santa Claus: twinkly, animated. Bits of chocolate were affixed to his beard. "Galloping camels. A foolish pleasure. But perhaps you're a fan."

"Not really," Cohen said.

"You look sad."

Cohen shook his head.

"You are far from home, I presume. What brings you here?"

"Business," Cohen said.

"Of what sort?"

"I don't mean to be rude." Cohen smiled in apology. "I really don't. But I'm thinking it might be best if I just had some quiet time."

The old man tapped his chin.

A few minutes later the sheik's nephew appeared. He glanced at the old man. "I see you've met the sheik," he said to Cohen.

THE SHEIK (AT LAST)

The sheik apologized to Cohen. He'd intended no deception. It was tradition, to see how a man behaves without the cloak of duty. This was at dinner, on the outskirts of the Emirate. They sat in an open courtyard, under torches, partaking from a large common bowl. The air was scented with cloves.

Cohen ate, miserably.

"You are unhappy," the sheik said.

"I'd just like to know—I realize you have customs, but I've been here for two days. It's been very nice. But I have a family at home, a young daughter, and I'd like to know, with all due respect." Cohen cleared his throat. "How can I help you?"

"Yes. Caution can descend into obscurity." The sheik scooped some rice into his mouth and chewed thoughtfully. "Tell me what investments you would advise in the event of an airborne disaster."

Cohen wasn't quite sure what he'd heard. Was it *urban*? "A disaster?" he said.

"A hijacking. Perhaps several. An attack on civilians initiated by airplanes." Cohen took a moment to gather himself. "That's not really my specialty," he said. "I work mostly with currency issues. Differentials. Perhaps there's been a misunderstanding."

The sheik continued to chew.

"We have an entire risk-assessment *division*," Cohen insisted.

"I know who you are," the sheik said. "And I am asking what *you* would advise."

Cohen gazed at the faint outline of a crane. "I'm not sure I feel comfortable answering that question."

The sheik regarded him with a warm smile. He was one of those men who exuded fatherly benevolence. It was probably nonsense. Probably he had his servants chopped in two for missing a spot. But it was difficult to feel that looking at him.

"I'd have to think about it," Cohen said.

SLIPPING BEAUTY

The avenues of the Emirate were wide and bright, and the construction never stopped. Workers swarmed and pecked and hammered. At night, lanterns hung from the rails and made the scaffolding wink. Cohen stood at his window in a cashmere bathrobe. His calls home had gone unanswered. It was Saturday night, Sunday morning. He wished he'd packed Chantal's sleeping pills.

He lay on the bed and considered calling his mother. She would think it was about Ruby. He would have to explain. *I'm in an Arab kingdom. No, Ma. It's for work. Yes, I'm eating.* He would tell her he was—what? Frightened? Lonely? The TV channels showed sports clips, models in bikinis, men burning things and laughing. Cohen didn't want to be any of them. But he didn't want to be himself, either. It was how TV got you.

In the middle of the night, he awoke to find a young woman sitting on the edge of his bed.

"Slipping beauty is awake," she said. Her accent was eastern European, comically so. The girl stood up and lifted her lingerie over her head. Her body, backlit by the TV, was a brutal sculpture. Her scapulae curved like dark wings. "Who do you want to be?" she declared. "We are outside of time."

Cohen's body understood the situation, but his mind was still foggy. The girl leaned toward the bed and made a purring noise. Her breasts shivered. The perfume hit hard. His fingers tensed, then a memory seized him, somewhat cruelly: his neighbor's eldest daughter, Julie Jewett, bending down to pull weeds. She was a plump, lascivious girl, snaggletoothed. A few years ago his mother had called with an urgent piece of gossip: Julie Jewitt had become (as she put it) a "streetwalker."

Cohen rubbed his eyes and the girl, the whore, was still there. "I appreciate the offer," he said. "I do. But I should sleep."

The girl began to touch herself. Her fingers made a wet click.

"Please. I have a wife and child."

"Lucky girls," she said.

Cohen gazed at the girl for another moment. Her face was immaculate, as if degradation were merely an inconvenient form of ambition. But she was too thin and too far from home. Her story wouldn't end well.

"Do you need help?" Cohen said.

The girl's neck stiffened. She looked as if she was going to spit at him.

"Please," he said again. "I'm just here for business."

DATA

He left a rather confused message for Mr. Vanderweghe and then inquired of the concierge as to the location of the American embassy. There wasn't a full embassy yet, just a few consular officers. He took a quick shower. When he emerged, the nephew was sitting on his couch, sucking on a fig.

"You got lunch plans?"

Cohen said, "I don't think that's a good idea."

"You're pissed about the girl, huh?"

Cohen shook his head, like it was all a misunderstanding. "I'm not the guy you want."

The nephew withdrew a PalmPilot from his robe and tapped a few buttons. "Daniel Evan Cohen. Born June 6, 1974. New Haven, Connecticut. Social security 421-90-5272."

Cohen's chest fluttered.

"Don't freak out," the sheik's nephew said. "The sheik just wants your advice."

"I don't really have a choice here, do I?"

The nephew looked offended. "You always have a choice," he said.

THE SHEIK (REDUX)

"I offer a second apology. It pains me to imagine a guest unhappy." The sheik plucked an olive from the colossal pile between them and began a dainty inspection. They were in a smaller courtyard. The frescoes along the walls shone violently.

"I appreciate that," Cohen said. "I really do. But I'm not sure—" He paused. "I feel like I might be being held against my will."

The sheik frowned. He tapped his heart with two fingers. "Nothing bad is going to happen to you, Daniel."

"But I could leave if I wanted? Right?"

"Of course." The sheik smoothed the robe over his belly. "Is this what you would like?"

Cohen filled his eyes with the utmost regret, and nodded.

"That is a disappointment to me," the sheik said. "I hoped we might become better acquainted. But I see I have given offense."

"It's only that I don't think I'm the best qualified to advise you."

"Yes," the sheik said. "You have told me there are others whose expertise exceeds yours. I understand. But you are the one who sits before me now." The sheik popped the olive into his mouth and licked his thumb. "Why do you think that is, Daniel?"

Cohen shook his head.

"Because I have chosen you."

"But you don't know me, really."

"I am coming to know you. I know, for one example, that you are worried about corruption. You regard it as an unnatural condition. It offends your morality. But what has been accomplished by our species that didn't involve foresight? Jacob and his birthright. David. Saul. We make the arrangements necessary to honor our covenants."

"I'm really only half-Jewish," Cohen said.

The sheik cast his eyes toward the blue square of sky above them and shrugged gently. "You may leave now, my friend. Of course. It was only a wish that you would serve as my adviser, not a command."

The sheik stood. Cohen was beset by a sudden confusion. He tried to gather himself, but could think only of his father returning home, dampened by rain, and the mood that seemed to blaze around him each night, which Cohen had always taken to be rage but which he now saw was something closer to panic. Once, when he was about ten, Cohen had found his father slumped in his recliner, staring out the window. "Do you want something, Dad?" Cohen said.

"A cold beer and a better life," his father said.

The sheik sank slowly back into his seat. He was still smiling, though his eyes were glum. "I am offering you an opportunity, Daniel. God bestowed certain talents upon you. I recognize them, even if you do not."

The question seemed to be: What sort of life did he feel himself entitled to? Wasn't that what the sheik was asking? Had his father ever been asked such a thing? Cohen's cheeks tingled. He felt a disorienting surge of relief.

"If I knew something were going to happen," he said softly, "a particular event, to a particular country. I'm speaking generally. You'd expect the currency to weaken, obviously. Certain industries would slump. Others would benefit over the long-term—defense for sure, private security—and you'd want to buy call options. You know what a call option is? You'd want to buy a whole bunch at a strike price that seemed insane. That'd be the way to do it, derivatives. Buy in volume through a series of offshores and sell off as you approach the strike. You load up on the stocks themselves, it's too fishy." Cohen paused. "What I'm telling you is what anyone could tell you."

"But you are not anyone," the sheik said. "You are Daniel Cohen."

FLIGHT

He was getting on a plane, escaping. He'd been chased through a series of atria by giant grouse, into a brightly lit tunnel that required him to hunch over. The tunnel turned into an airport terminal, a tarmac, and now this plane where he sat with something bundled in his arms that he wasn't allowed to look at. The engines coughed to life and he closed his eyes. The pilot's voice came over the intercom and it was Mr. Santello, his father's boss. "We've got a problem up here," he said.

Cohen opened his eyes. The dawn was a red blade over the Gulf.

THE SHEIK (A FINAL TIME)

His office was in a small, anonymous building several miles from the city center. It was humbler than Cohen expected. On one wall were photos of the sheik: flanked by two senators, shaking hands with a vice president, gazing shyly at a young pop star as she sipped from a straw. The singer's mysterious death had been ruled a suicide.

Cohen didn't hear the sheik come in.

"Sit sit sit," he said. "You look tired, Daniel. Did you sleep?"

"Some," Cohen said.

"Strange dreams? It happens when I travel. But Daniel is the one who understands dreams, is he not?"

"I'd like to leave," Cohen said. "You said yesterday I could leave if I wanted to."

The sheik looked pleased. "He comes to the court of the Babylonians to advise the king. I don't suppose Daniel was any happier among the Chaldeans. Then the den of lions. Terrifying! Even for a man of great faith."

Cohen had a wild notion: the sheik was himself a dream. The towers and minarets—none of it was real. Soon Ruby, summoned from a fitful sleep, would cry out. He would find her curled against the rail of her crib, rubbing her eyes in the dim.

The sheik said, "Let me tell you what will happen next. The nominal sum that resides with your current firm will remain there. A larger sum will be transferred to a fund and placed under your sole control." The sheik mentioned a sum.

Cohen went white.

"There will be no records, paper or otherwise," the sheik said. "Your namesake, in addition to his talent with dreams, was an exceptional administrator. This is why the sultans employed Jews for financial matters. Jews feel an ethical compulsion. They are, you might say, honest despite themselves."

"I've been with the company less than six months," Cohen said.

The sheik tossed his hands in sympathy.

"What about Mr. Vanderweghe?"

"You musn't worry about him."

"My wife. She told me this might happen."

"Yes, Chantal is it? Shall we call her?"

The sheik took the phone and murmured a few words in Arabic, then jabbed a button and Chantal's quavery voice rang out.

"Allo? Allo?"

"*Honey?*" Cohen said.

The sheik excused himself from the room with a small bow.

"How did you get on this phone line?" Cohen said.

"You called me," Chantal said. "Why do you yell?"

"I want to know what the fuck is going on."

But Cohen could see the situation. The sheik had hired Chantal to seduce him. How hard would that have been? Cohen with his bulging eyes and his nose. She had worn a white sarong the first time he saw her. And now she had a child, his child, his Ruby, and he was bound to do right by both of them.

"How much did they pay you?" he said.

"Dan'el—"

"Don't lie to me," Cohen said.

Chantal began weeping, not the loud sobs of an actress, but soft squealing hiccups, like a dolphin. She sounded like Ruby, that pure in her misery. She had been this way the night she confessed her pregnancy—a former exchange student of dubious means adrift in America, standing in the middle of Cohen's living room, shivering, her teeth stained by the wine she had drunk to muster her nerve.

"I'm sorry," Cohen said.

"I don't unnerstan."

"Don't listen to me," Cohen said. "I'm just tired."

"What do you mean who pays me?"

Cohen closed his eyes. "I made a mistake. The hours have been very long here and I haven't been sleeping well. I got confused."

Chantal blew her nose. "When are you coming home?"

"Soon. Tomorrow probably."

"We miss you," Chantal said.

Her voice was so soft. "I miss you, too. I miss you both." He would grow old with this woman, her needy aggravations, the way she clung to Ruby as the child fed from her breast.

"Dan'el? Are you okay?"

"Yeah. Don't worry. I'll be home soon." Cohen paused. "Listen, I may get a promotion."

EXIT STRATEGY

Cohen was in a limo. His bags were in the back. Someone else had packed them.

"You deal with me now," the nephew said. He sipped from a snifter of fresh orange juice and something else. "Look: There's nothing you can do about any of this shit. It's happening way above your head. It's happening in some cave you've never even thought about."

Cohen shook his head. "It doesn't make sense. You don't need me."

"Probably not," the nephew said. "But you're a loyal guy. Not everyone is like that anymore. You take care of your family and you do good work at your job, which happens to be making money on investments. It doesn't sound like a bad life, man. Anyway, it wasn't my call."

They drove on in silence. Cohen watched the desert flick past.

"You think we control shit, but we don't," the nephew said. "We didn't put the plankton under the earth. We didn't invent the car or the highway or the dollar." He was a drunk, sociably so. "That kind of luck can't last forever, right? So you diversify. No one's going to plant drugs in your bag or mess with your kid or listen in on your phone calls. Stop worrying. It's just business."

MANKIND

Cohen stared out his window. The plane banked sharply and the latest of the Sura Islands came into view. Workers swarmed over the sand like dark insects.

The sheik had made a gift to him of a bilingual Koran, and

Cohen spent a few minutes flipping around in the book, trying to identify the islands before they slid from view.

One of his servers, the loveliest, knelt beside him. "Al-Nas," she whispered.

"I'm sorry?" Cohen said.

She blushed. "The final sura."

"What's it mean?"

"Look it up," she said playfully.

Cohen struggled to look away from her, from the idea—painfully clear to him—that he could have her if he so desired. He glanced at the Koran.

"Mankind," she said. "We ask Allah for protection from Satan." She held out her hand and Cohen handed her the book and she turned to the right page and handed it back, so Cohen could see it in English.

The girl closed her eyes and began singing in Arabic.

In the name of Allah, the Beneficent, the Merciful.
Say: I seek refuge in the Lord of Mankind.
The King of Mankind.
The God of Mankind.
From the evil of the sneaking whisperer.
Who whispereth in the hearts of mankind.
Of the jinn and of mankind.

The girl finished singing and opened her eyes. The plane banked again and she set her hand on Cohen's shoulder and squeezed lightly.

"Who is the jinn?" Cohen said.

"You would say, maybe, 'genie.' A powerful ghost. Something you cannot see that holds you."

The girl asked if he wanted anything else.

Cohen shook his head slowly. He looked down at the page again and read the words and tried to imagine a God equal to the trouble of His creation. The plane hit a patch of bad air and for a moment Cohen was plummeting toward the earth, a small creature, smaller than Ruby, whistling with dumb velocity. When he awoke, the jeweled lights of his city were beneath him. *So this is who I am*, he thought.

Cohen had asked his father once whether God existed. He wanted to know if it was God who lifted your body into heaven when you died. "What you see is what you get," his father said. It was true, like most things his father said, which made it no less cruel.

FIRST DATE BACK

IN THE GATE AREA Sanchez started chanting his fight song again. He and the others had been at it since Frankfurt, where they'd fanned out with their vouchers and returned bellowing with pilsner. They were in the Atlanta airport now—carpeted halls, the soft hum of commerce—back in the custody of Uncle Sammy, two hours into their lives as veterans of a foreign war.

Tedesco wanted Sanchez to sit down, shut up, show some dignity. But he was nineteen years old, tanked up on the drama; all the fat civilians jammed into their leather seats were watching him. "No more hajji," Sanchez sang, "no more prayer! No more dirty hajji air!" A few folks looked away. One guy, an old dude in a golf shirt, began to clap. Then the gate agent clicked on her mic and said, "We'd like to welcome some very *special* travelers home," and the entire gate area burst into applause. Everyone was smiling at them so hard. Tedesco let himself feel the joy of the moment and it stung.

They boarded right after first class. It was a midday flight, half-empty. Tedesco stepped onto the plane and saw a flight attendant bent over in the galley, the broad curve of her sheathed in a dark blue skirt. Then she rose and turned and looked at him—they were inches apart—and Tedesco fell dumb in love.

He knew this was absurd, but he also knew what he felt, the fierce tug inside. Her skin was tan and her mouth was full, though it was her eyes that startled him: a pale green rimmed in clumpy mascara. He saw the surrender there, the gentle acceptance of human sadness. It made his throat constrict.

"Welcome aboard," she said shyly.

As they taxied, she did the safety instructions. He watched her work the seat belt buckle and the oxygen mask; he watched her hands. She was bored but careful. If the engines blew and the plane went screaming down, she'd be in charge. She held the plastic safety card in front of her face and Tedesco thought of the women he'd seen in the hajji markets, the way their eyes settled on a man before shifting back to the piles of dried fruit.

"See something you like?" Hayes elbowed him.

"Zip it," Tedesco said.

Hayes grinned innocently and cranked his iPod. Tedesco could hear the distant tin rage. The shit his guys listened to. He liked the old stuff, Dion and the Belmonts, "Runaround Sue," the sound track of his uncle's barbershop. The guys called him "Old-Timer" and "Frank," as in Sinatra, which was another thing altogether, though you couldn't make them understand that.

The flight attendant, his attendant, was making her way through the cabin with the cart, serving drinks, while her old-crow partner did pretzels. She was a big girl, with round hips and a small chest. It only made her more beautiful. She looked like a real girl, not porn.

Tedesco ordered a root beer and she smiled and blushed and that made him blush, too.

"We don't have root beer."

"Coke is fine."

The attendant set his Coke down and Hayes said, "Ma'am, just so you know—"

But Tedesco could see he was about to say something stupid— *Sarge here thinks you're a knockout*, or *This is Tommy, you should see his salami*—and he put an elbow into his sternum. Hayes began quietly convulsing for air. They didn't know how to act around women. They knew how to clean their guns and line a perimeter, but there was a lot of stuff still missing.

"He's fine," Tedesco said. "Just get him a beer."

It took Hayes a minute to get his breath back. "Shit," he said. "We're home, man. You can relax." Hayes grabbed his beer and went to sit with Sanchez and the others a few rows up. They ordered cheap Scotch in tiny bottles and made sentimental toasts. "To us and those who want to be like us," Sanchez yelled. Their scalps shone over the seat backs like stubbled eggs. Tedesco closed his eyes and tried to imagine his mother, hugging his mother, but he couldn't make the image resolve.

Someone was touching his shoulder. He opened his eyes. She was standing over him, holding a miniature bottle of wine. Her wrists smelled of old roses. "This is for you," she said. "Your friends bought it for you." Her voice was a little husky, the vowels flattened out. Midwestern.

Sanchez and the rest of them were staring back.

Her beauty was crippling. He wanted to say just the right thing.

"That's funny," he said. "They were joking."

The girl smiled uncertainly. "But they paid for it. It's paid for."

"Do you like white wine?"

"We're not allowed."

Sanchez made a hooting noise and the girl turned.

"Sorry," Tedesco said. "We're just back. A lot of the guys, they're kind of excited. Sorry about that."

The girl smiled again. How old was she? Tedesco had no idea. He wished he were handsome, that he could offer her a face worthy of hers. But he was who he was, Tommy Tedesco, with the crooked nose and the eyebrows. He was a monster.

"That's okay." The girl touched his shoulder and slipped the bottle into her apron. "I'm off duty when we land."

Tedesco knew this meant nothing. It was what women did here. They were allowed to flirt. They gathered male attention around themselves. He couldn't help wondering, though. They were flying into Newark. No one was meeting him at the airport, because he hadn't told his mom. He didn't want a big production, all the aunts and cousins, the homemade desserts and flags and questions.

Maybe he could ask her to dinner. He could hit the assistance button and she would come over and he would say, "Would you like to get some dinner?" But there were good-byes to consider. Hayes and the others in his unit would want him to meet their families: *This is our sarge, he's a real hard-ass. Just kidding, Sarge!* The prospect exhausted him. He wanted the girl. He wanted to climb into her body and never come out.

THE PLANE LANDED and Tedesco decided to speak to her, a quick, low-key invite. She had told him she was off duty. She had touched his shoulder. He wasn't imagining things. He made his way to the front of the plane. The edge of her uniform peeked out from the galley. His heart was beating all stupid. He kept his gaze averted. His uncles had taught him that. *Your eyes should surprise her, like a breeze under the skirt.* Then he reached her and looked and it was the old crow. The girl, his girl, must have been behind him, in the jump seat at the rear of the plane. Shit luck.

Hayes and the other guys were waiting for him in the terminal.

That was how it had been over there. You felt safe with other guys around, even though the brass told you not to congregate. They were drunk and nervous. You could see it in their big, swooping steps. Tedesco kept his back straight, but he wished he were out of uniform. Then they hit the security gate and the clapping started again. Their relatives were waving homemade signs. Reichart ran ahead with Thorpe. They picked up their mothers and twirled them around. Cameras flashed. Tedesco smiled. He wanted to feel the way he was supposed to feel.

They had girls, too, sweet, embarrassed little things. Sanchez pinned his against a wall. She was pregnant and weepy, with dark eyes and a spray of acne across her forehead. Sanchez whispered Spanish as he groped her.

Strangers kept coming up to Tedesco. They wanted to shake his hand and say thank you. They stared into his eyes with self-satisfied reverence. It was like he'd performed some unpleasant task for them, and now they were square.

At baggage claim, he said good-bye to his guys. He made earnest, vacant promises, waited for them to clear out, then hoisted the duffel across his shoulders. He'd asked to terminate at Newark so he could take the train to Providence, give himself some time to adjust. He stood near the exit but couldn't bring himself to step outside. The night seemed a little too dark, too crowded. A river of headlights cast shadows on the dingy concrete. Tedesco kneeled on his duffel.

He closed his eyes and before he could get them open again he was back at the checkpoint outside Samarra and it was night and an old man in white was running toward him and he was calling out for the man to stop, to show his hands, lift your fucking hands, and his gun was drawn and he could smell diesel and see bluish pricks of light on the horizon and the man was carrying something and he wouldn't raise his arms and he wouldn't stop.

Tedesco felt a thud, then a hand on his shoulder. A soft voice said, "Are you all right? Officer Tedesco?"

He opened his eyes and she was there, the attendant, his girl.

Her brow was creased with an exquisite worry. Tedesco looked around. They were in the Newark airport. His forehead had fallen against a cement pillar.

"Fine," he said. "I'm fine." He waited for the small crowd behind her to disperse.

"You don't seem fine," she said. A plump blue bag stood beside her.

"Long trip," Tedesco said. "I was a little more tired than I realized."

She drew back slightly, as if to appraise him. Her eyes were pinched mournfully at the corners. The purse slung over her shoulder disturbed the fabric just enough to reveal the edge of a bra strap. Black.

"Let me buy you dinner," Tedesco said suddenly.

She narrowed her eyes. "Are you going to be okay?"

"I will be if you join me for dinner. I might not make it otherwise."

"You don't seem well. You were staggering."

"A beautiful woman does that to me."

Tedesco felt oddly buoyant. This was what it was like to work a woman, the sweet con of flattery. He'd almost forgotten. The lessons imparted by his uncles meant nothing over there. The female soldiers didn't care to dance. They were practical.

"Where's your family?" she said.

"Tomorrow. It's all arranged. I'm going to surprise my mom." Tedesco straightened up. He was no taller than she was, probably an inch shorter. It hadn't been so noticeable on the plane. He didn't mind. He liked her size, the great shape of her. He wanted to take her hand. "Have dinner with me," Tedesco said. "You're off duty, right?"

"Coffee," she said. "Maybe a coffee."

HER NAME WAS VALERIE. She was from Elkhart, Indiana. Her dad had been the coach of the girls' basketball team, on which she had played all four years, though she'd also been a runner-up for prom queen, a fact she mentioned with some embarrassment only after Tedesco pressed. She had been a flight attendant for two years. She wanted to see the world. But foreign routes were based on seniority, so it might be twenty years before she got herself assigned to Europe. Mostly, she said, she saw airports and hotel lobbies. She was twenty-four years old.

Tedesco said he understood. He'd considered the army for much the same reason. He had a friend, Andruzzi, over in Germany, who told him you could go anywhere you wanted if you could arrange transport. Paris. Amsterdam. Brussels. Then 9/11 happened and he'd felt, you know, there was a greater responsibility to the whole thing now.

Tedesco didn't tell her that he'd actually enlisted three weeks before 9/11, that he'd done so because he could see that if he stayed in Providence he'd wind up with a shitty muni job (his uncle Gus had connections with public works) and his mother's nagging. He didn't even like to think this way. He loved his mother. She had suffered enough. He could take care of her now. The prospect sickened him.

They shared a taxi to her hotel, the Marriott. He told her he had a room there, too, total coincidence, so she wouldn't think he was some kind of stalker. It wasn't just physical desire. There was something blooming inside him. He asked her again, in the lobby, to have dinner with him.

"I'm supposed to meet some of the girls," she said.

"You can see them anytime," Tedesco said. The darkness outside loomed. He had pills to put himself to sleep, but it kept taking more and more to get him down and he woke to the world groggy and alarmed.

Her reluctance was obvious, so he stepped back and bowed his head. It was the same gesture he had seen his uncles make in the face of a debt collector. "I'm sorry," he said. "I don't mean to push. I'm out of practice with this stuff. Women and all. Life in the army isn't too great for the social graces. You already have plans. I understand." He looked down and waited a second or two.

"I'd have to change," she said finally.

THEY ATE AT THE HOTEL RESTAURANT. It was called Piccadilly Circus, which was a famous shopping district in London that Valerie wanted to visit. She had changed into a yellow summer dress, and a gray cardigan. Her hair was pinned up and she wore thick glasses now. She looked like a schoolteacher. Tedesco had changed into his dress pants and a white button-down, both of which he had ironed in his room. He felt less noticeable out of uniform, though he thought maybe Valerie was disappointed. They were civilians now. They might be a young couple on the eve of a romantic getaway.

She ate with surprising vigor, but when he gently teased her about this she flushed and set her fork down.

"I'm sorry," Tedesco said. "I was just kidding around. I think it's great that you know how to enjoy a meal. Seriously. Most girls, they don't eat anything in front of a guy. They think they should be these little twigs. It's unhealthy. Unnatural. A woman should look like a woman." He paused. "Look, like I told you, I'm full of stupid comments. But please don't take offense. As far as I'm concerned, you look about as perfect as someone could look."

She flushed again and excused herself.

Tedesco watched her as she rose from the table, the thin fabric of her dress. He closed his eyes and imagined running his hand across her belly. He felt weak and stupid with his intentions.

She took longer than he expected. Had she abandoned him? He'd taken a Xanax before dinner and now he took another, to keep his mind from running in the wrong direction. He was famished, but the thought of eating nauseated him.

She returned to the table and sat down. "Thank you for dinner, Tom. I should probably go now."

"Wait a second," Tedesco said. "Wait."

"I have a boyfriend," she said quickly. "I should have told you earlier."

"That's fine," he said. "We're just having dinner. I'm not trying to steal you away from someone. I just wanted to talk with you. Look, just consider yourself a coach, someone to help me adjust to the dating world again."

"You don't seem to need coaching."

"You're wrong about that," Tedesco said. "Look at it: first I make some dumb crack about your eating. Then I apologize by announcing how perfect you look. I overdo it. I'm not doing so good." This was something his uncle Fiorello said to women. *I'm not doing so good.* It had a magical effect.

"WHAT WAS IT LIKE OVER THERE?" she asked.

They were in the bar now, surrounded by businessmen and the sullen, gliding staff. He was drinking beer and she had ordered a second martini, which she was nursing.

Tedesco was surprised it had taken her so long to ask. "Like being a cop in a crappy neighborhood, I guess. Not so different from here."

"It's not dangerous?"

"Everywhere is dangerous. Working on an airplane is dangerous."

"Not really," she said. "We've only had one commercial crash in the past decade, if you don't count 9/11."

"Big if."

"It's more than two thousand times safer than riding in a car."

Tedesco's father had died in a car wreck. Tedesco, who was four at the time, remembered him as a friendly man in a dark uniform that smelled of smoke. He was a fireman, the family hero. And a drunk driver, as his mother never failed to note. "A good heart don't mean shit," she told Tedesco, "if you make bad decisions."

Valerie was looking at him intently, worried again, so Tedesco smiled quickly and said, "So what, no close calls?

"I had a girl who had an allergic reaction to something once," Valerie said. "We were worried her throat might get blocked. But Diane gave her a shot from the first aid kit and she was fine." She stared at her drink, trying to decide whether to ask. "Did you have any over there?" she said. "Close calls?"

Tedesco shook his head. "Be honest with you, I was mostly doing supply op. Coordinating food transfers. An army marches on its stomach. You wouldn't believe how much chow we distributed over there. Our warehouse was the size of an airport hangar."

"Isn't it mostly just MREs?"

"That's for the grunts. But you've got a whole civilian authority over there, media center, command staff. We had steaks, shrimp, lobster, chicken cordon bleu, wine, fresh fruits and vegetables. The Bounty, we called it. The REMFs would come in there and order straight off the shelves."

Valerie wrinkled her nose. "REMFs?"

"That's what we called the rear echelon guys."

Those two months in supply req had fucked with his head. He would pass from the Bounty into the streets, where everyone— the hajjis, the hajji widows, the little hajji kids in their raggedy T-shirts—looked hot and underfed and dirty, and wanted to beg but wouldn't. The teenagers stood around bombed-out buildings, drinking tea and smoking their shitty cigs, trying to decide which way to lean in their plastic dress shoes. Tedesco felt like the shopkeeper in a dying mill town.

"You never had to go out on patrol or anything?" Valerie said.

"You're thinking Vietnam. Iraq is different."

"You never shot at anyone or anything?"

"Sorry to disappoint you."

"I'm not disappointed. I was just wondering."

"Sure." They all wanted war stories. It was why he and the

others had been sent over there in the first place: to bear the awful things close to death and to return with stories. This is what sustained the folks back home, brought them out of their stupor, closer to life. They were vampires.

"You're mad at me," Valerie said.

He looked at the pale flesh of her throat and downed his beer. "Sorry," he said. "I got upset. I'm bad at this. Let's talk about something else."

Some old love song, reduced to synthesized mush, poured from the speakers above them. A group of women, lavishly made-up, sailed through the lobby on a gale of forced laughter. Tedesco inspected his face in the dark glass that divided their booth from the next one and grimaced.

He asked her questions that felt significant and listened vaguely to her answers. He told her he wanted to become a paramedic. He spoke of his loyalty to his ill mother. He mentioned a few of the things he had seen—the orphan kids who jumped from the top of the Paradise Hotel onto mattresses in the alley below, the grief-stricken woman who set her chickens on fire, one by one. But he could tell she wanted to go. She refused a third drink. She yawned behind her fist. She told him, finally, that she needed to call someone. She had promised.

"Sure," Tedesco said. "I get it."

"This was nice," she said. "I'm sure you'll make a great paramedic."

She fiddled with her purse, but he shook his head. "Don't worry about it," he said, as sweetly as he could manage. "Seriously. I appreciate the company. Go make your call."

He watched the sway of her bottom, hungrily, pathetically, until it was gone. Back in his room, he drank two more beers from the minibar and took an Ambien, but he couldn't sleep. Not with her in the same hotel. He was in love with her, he was pretty sure. He lay on his bed and saw her face, then tried to forget it. They were destined, she just didn't realize it yet. He went to the bathroom and sat on the can and stared at the sports pages and tried to attach some concern to the teams he had loved as a boy. He opened the blinds and looked at the lights of Newark. They were yellowish-white here and laid out in neat rows. He called down to reception and got her number and dialed before he could stop himself.

She fumbled with the receiver.

"It's Tom," he said. "Tom Tedesco. Were you sleeping?"

"Sort of."

"I'm sorry. I didn't mean to disturb you. I know you have a boyfriend. I just wanted to say that I had a great time this evening. Talking. I think you're a special person and I felt I had to say that, because I don't know that I'll ever see you again. I don't mean to be all dramatic, but it's true."

"You sound funny."

"I'm a little upset, I guess. Not feeling so good. It's weird to be back."

Valerie sighed. He waited for her to say something.

"I'm not sure I should be alone right now," he said.

SHE ENTERED THE LOBBY in a baggy sweater and jeans. Her face, scrubbed of its makeup, looked puffy and impatient. They sat in the chairs near the revolving door.

"Thanks for coming," he said, as if they were at a wake.

"What's going on, exactly?"

Tedesco laughed a little. "Just nerves, you know. Another drink might help. We could get another drink."

"Do you think you might want to talk to someone? Like a professional?"

Tedesco looked her in the face until she looked away. His arms flexed, then his legs. "This sounds crazy. But I felt something toward you, a special thing. It happened the moment I saw you on the plane. I know how this sounds, but it happens sometimes. It happened to my uncle. He saw his wife, and he felt if he could hold her, life would make sense." He swallowed. "I thought you might understand."

Valerie was looking at him calmly. "So you want to hold me?"

Tedesco nodded meekly.

"Despite the fact that you don't know me, and I don't know you. Despite the fact that I have a boyfriend. You feel you have the right to call me at one in the morning and say these things to me?" Her tone had some steel now: the coach's daughter.

Tedesco had a vision of her naked, in a gym, her big brown body with all its curves reflected in the hardwood. He wanted to take hold of her. He wanted permission. "What does your boyfriend do?" he said.

"We're not going to talk about that."

Tedesco looked down. "It's because I'm ugly," he said.

"No. You're not listening. There's no *it* between us. You're a sweet guy. I'm flattered. But you're confused. You need to see your family . . ." She continued to speak, in her new, adult voice. It made Tedesco want to put his hand over her mouth and pull off her sweater. He couldn't make the impulse go away. It jittered inside him.

"I'm just back, all right. I'm confused. But I'm not a kid. I saw you and I knew. Why can't you accept that?"

Valerie was looking at him in a manner Tedesco couldn't quite figure.

"Some homecoming," he said.

"You need to see your family," she repeated.

"I'm just back," he said. "From the war."

"That doesn't have anything to do with me."

"Yes it does." Tedesco clenched his jaw. His tone was imploring. "Why do you think I was over there?"

Valerie looked toward the reception desk. The overnight clerk was gone. "You didn't really have a room booked here, did you, Tom?" she said.

Tedesco clasped his hands together, to keep them still. "Whatever happened to 'Support the Troops'?" He tried to smile, but his throat ached and his stupid eyes had pooled up. "Shit." He bowed his head and said, very softly, "I'm sorry. I'm sorry, Valerie. I didn't mean to get like this. Nights aren't so good for me." It was a sad ploy, this begging. He hated himself for enlisting her in his suffering. It was what men did. They charged toward doom and presented their ruined selves for repair. His army shrink, a bigmouth Jew from Scranton, had told him this.

"You're frightened," she said. "It's nothing to be ashamed of."

Tedesco kept saying, "You must think I'm crazy."

No, she said, that wasn't it. He was just under a lot of pressure. She helped him calm down and agreed to walk him to his room. She did this in exchange for a promise that he would talk to someone, a professional, in the morning.

At the door to his room he turned to thank her. "I wanted to give you something," he said.

"Tomorrow," she said. "At breakfast."

He opened the door with his room card but for some reason he had left the lights off. The room was dark and he stood in the doorway and stared out the window; the lights of Newark seemed fainter now. He could have switched on the light. His hand was right there. But he remained in the dark and let his mind wander off, go AWOL.

The old hajji was running toward him, holding something against his chest, refusing to raise his hands. Tedesco kept shouting for him to stop, in Arabic, in English; he fired a shot into the air but the old man kept coming right up the center of the highway. Benson should have been there to light him up with one of their portable kliegs, but he was taking a pisser so Tedesco was on his own and he aimed a second shot over the man's head and the man paused for a second, then started forward again. Tedesco couldn't see what he was carrying and their CO had reminded them to use extreme caution when it came to vehicles or men on foot, you didn't know who was who at night and any American was a target and these guys—the jihadi—hell, they *wanted* to die with you. That was how they got to heaven. All the parts that exploded on earth got mended up in heaven and virgins held you in their arms for the rest of time. One of them was speaking now, saying his name softly: *Tom? Tom?*

Tedesco tried to warn her, to get her away in time, but the man wouldn't stop and he had something in his arms, one of those homemade IEDs, full of gunpowder and glass, nails, whatever. The man had cased them, a couple of Americans at a remote checkpoint, and pounced. What other explanation could there be? If it looks like a duck and walks like a duck. Tedesco didn't have a lot of time to consider his options. The old man was wailing now. The white of his robe sliced the night. He was fifty yards off at most. His sandals slapped the pavement. If he got within twenty you could expect the worst. A guy Tedesco knew, a fat lieutenant, had strolled into the wrong lobby just as a hajji porter detonated himself and the guy had wound up with shards of skull, fucking skull, stuck in his gut.

Tedesco turned away from his room toward the bright hall, and she nearly rescued him. If she had looked at him right then with anything like love—not even love, but the forgiveness she guarded within her. He wanted to fall backward, out of the blackness. But he was frozen inside his body. The old man kept coming, so close now that Tedesco could see his hands curled tenderly around the bomb, and Tedesco unloaded a third shot at his feet and the white spark flashed and it was clear the man was trying to murder him, he was screaming with that holy wish and Tedesco had to convince himself: he wants you dead, *this guy wants you dead*, he needed his brain to understand and send the message to his eyes and his trigger finger and then it had happened and the man went down with a soft thud and Tedesco realized that it wasn't the old man who had been screaming, but him.

Benson called the incident in and HQ dispatched an IED unit. He and Benson had orders to stay away from the body; the bomb might be live. A pair of specialists arrived. Tedesco didn't see what happened next. Benson was still talking to him ("You did the right thing, Sarge, saved our fucking asses") when they heard one of the specialists shout "Fuck." Benson, who was part of his crew, a subordinate, told him to stay put and went out there and when he came back his dark face looked chalky.

"What?" Tedesco said.

One of the guys from the IED unit appeared in the doorway. "Time for you to go," he said.

"What the hell?" Tedesco turned back and saw the bodies laid out in the phosphorous light of flares: the old man on his side and the baby next to him, a dark puddle circling both. A medic crouched over the baby and tried to stanch one part of its chest while jabbing a needle into the tiny arm.

"Is that what I did?" Tedesco said.

"You didn't do shit," one of the other IED guys said. "You did your job, okay?"

VALERIE KEPT REPEATING THE WORD. "Okay? Okay?" She should have walked away, gotten clear of the blast radius. He wanted to warn her. But she kept hovering there. It made a man expect solace. The light of the hallway glared down upon him and she was a vision: her hips and her breasts and her mouth and her neck. He saw her in a white dress, on a green lawn, swollen with life. He wanted to be held by her. He wanted to climb inside. His muscles twitched. He stepped into the light and her body was as soft as he wished it to be.

"Calm down, Tom. I don't—"

Her perfume offered some imitation of flowers. Her bones were an inconvenience. He worked around them.

"Stop," she said. "*Now.*"

A strong girl, a big healthy American girl, not an angel, but close, some version of the thing.

"Don't do this."

He needed her inside. There was no other way. Her eyes were a blurry sea and her belly was a smooth field and he could smell her better now, not the flowers but the soil beneath, to which all foolish bodies return, and he carried her over the threshold, into the black silence, searching frantically for the part of her that would subdue his terror, accept his love, save him.

A DREAM OF SLEEP

THE CARETAKER'S NAME WAS WOLF PINKAS. He lived with his two cats in a stone cottage at the rear of the cemetery. The building, a square structure six feet high, had been erected as a family crypt. But the wealthy Prussian immigrant who commissioned it disappeared without a trace before the First World War. Unable to sell the vault, the owners of the cemetery, a family named Gardner, converted it to a caretaker's shed.

In the decade following World War II, when Wolf assumed the position of caretaker, the yard was a thriving concern. Its high walls shimmered with ivy; dainty wood benches lined its paths. The graves were in the eastern European fashion, aboveground, great slabs of marble or slate etched with names and dates and inlaid with small circular photos of the deceased. On weekends and holidays, relatives came to set out flowers, votive candles, wreaths of hazelnut. They carried picnic lunches and sat on the benches and ate and laughed with the dead.

But the yard had fallen from prosperity. The elder Gardner died, leaving management to his son, a young man with slicked-back hair who informed Wolf he no longer had the funds to pay for both caretaking services and security.

Wolf was a shy man, unaccustomed to speech. His face reddened and his hands, unusually large for a man who stood barely five feet, began to tremble. "Them visitors," he said slowly, hoping to undo the effects of his heavy accent, "what will they do?"

"No one's buying plots," the young Gardner murmured. "I'm sorry, Mr. Pinkas."

The implication was clear: Wolf would have to find work elsewhere. The thought sent dread scouring through him. After some hesitation, he declared he would take a pay reduction in exchange for permission to move into the shed.

Gardner glanced at the crypt and broke into a grin. "But you're still a young man, Pinkas. You might want . . . company."

Wolf's throat constricted. He knew Gardner found his proposal morbid, but Gardner was an American. He understood the body as an object of desire. He had been spared a true accounting of the world, its rancid plains and oceans of tormented flesh. Only the dead were safe.

"It will not be a problem," Wolf said.

Gardner pursed his thin lips. "You'd have to double as security," he said at last.

Wolf, who was frightened of weapons and their use, quietly assented.

The young man removed a small whisk brush from his coat pocket and dusted his wing tips. "Nothing but ghosts in this place anyway, right?"

"I hope," Wolf said.

The shed had never been intended as a domicile and Wolf spent an entire autumn making it habitable. He purchased a potbellied stove from an estate sale, placed a tin basin beside it for bathing, drilled holes in the roof for ventilation, built a privy out back, and conveyed the few furnishings from his nearby apartment. The architect of the crypt had been thoughtful enough to include several arched window slots, intended for stained glass, and Wolf constructed wooden shutters for them. On cold nights he bolted the shutters and unplugged his tiny refrigerator from the portable generator and attached a heater. In the warm months he left the shutters open and breezes stirred the room's air.

Wolf spent his days as he always had, clearing vines from footpaths, hacking at the weeds that encroached upon remote plots. Waxed paper bags and wrappers drifted in from the street out front, where there was a trolley stop, and found their way into corners of the yard. Wolf made a round before sundown, jabbing them with a wooden spear he had fashioned for this purpose. He worked methodically to preserve the rightful peace accorded the dead.

At night he listened to classical music, Chopin mostly, Mozart and Bach, played on an ancient crank phonograph. It was his lone concession to the past, for his father, Dr. Pinkas, had loved Chopin, the fragile nocturnes, the rousing mazurkas. These were the songs he would hum to Wolf and his older sisters at night and, later, in the dim chaos of the boxcars and roads. Wolf lay on his cot and closed his eyes. The nocturnes made him weep, quietly and with some relief.

He ate lightly. Tea and toast in the mornings, fruit at lunch, a sandwich with soup for supper. He treated his cats to a bit of meat each day. He had not intended to keep pets. No, the cats had come to him. Dempsey was a large orange tom with frayed ears and a left eye that had been battered into a rakish wink. Coal, a skeletal black kitten, had arrived on a frosty morning and immediately, to the distress of all involved parties, attempted to suckle Dempsey.

Each month a small check signed by young Gardner was slipped into the mailbox outside the gate. The next morning

Wolf walked the half mile to his bank, where he cashed his check and then continued on to the barber and grocer.

When the bank and barber closed, he climbed onto a trolley to do his errands. Then the city's trolley service ceased, its tracks ripped from the ground and piled about. Asphalt and pavement seemed to wash outward from the roads, welcoming a greater flow of cars. Tar fouled the air. Wires snarled overhead. In the near distance, cranes pieced together the skeletons of skyscrapers. No matter how neatly men striped the center of the streets, no matter how bright the billboard promises, disorder hurtled on. Wolf ventured out less and then less.

Frail figures still appeared in the cemetery, occasionally seeking Wolf out to praise the upkeep of the yard and the garden he had coaxed from the sandy soil around his cottage. Wolf nodded at these comments and smiled and disappeared from view as courteously as possible.

But these older visitors, who understood the importance of spending a few hours each week in the company of the dead, died off themselves. Though there were still unfilled plots for sale, their younger relatives buried them closer to their own neighborhoods, in suburban cemeteries that looked to Wolf like a species of park, acres of grass smoothed of unsightly wrinkles. Small stone tablets marked the graves, or discreet plaques of the sort used elsewhere to announce historical sites. A road wound through the indistinguishable rows, for those who sought a whiff of the dead as they drove past.

The decline in visitors increased Wolf's workload, as the care of individual plots, which had once been the assumed duty of relatives, now passed to him. It was he who ensured that headstones were kept free of rubbish, the photos polished, the dead flowers cleared away. He enjoyed these tasks, which seemed to him the logical completion of a cycle to which he had given his life over contentedly.

Wolf was not a man prone to fancy. But sometimes, as he hunched to clean a sheet of marble or set a bouquet of wildflowers at the foot of a favorite grave, he heard a faint voice on the breeze. Once in a great while, these apparitions materialized outside his cottage and hovered in the moonlight. When he played Mozart, they waltzed with cautious grace. The cats perched on the sill and watched.

After a lengthy period of construction, the road fronting the cemetery became a four-lane highway, and thereafter the surrounding neighborhood declined precipitously. Private homes were demolished and large, drab public-housing projects built. During the cold months, after supper, Wolf lay on his cot and read, the cats flung atop him like pelts. But when the nights turned warm, Wolf could hear young blacks in the park next door, laughter and shouts, bottles shattering against the cemetery's brick walls, the snap of firecrackers, which frightened the cats. Graffiti surfaced on the walls near the front gate. Wolf considered apprising Gardner of the problem, but decided to purchase additional paint instead.

Gardner was a busy man and his annual visits lasted barely long enough for Wolf to count the buttons shining on his coat. "Sales have been a bit off," he observed. "Orders will come up by winter." With a sour expression, he would then inquire if anything was needed, to which Wolf would respond, with a slight bow, in the negative.

One evening, after closing, a tall figure in a sagging suit presented himself at the gate. He let himself in with a key and tromped about the place with a tape measure in one hand and a notepad in the other, so engrossed that he failed to notice Wolf's approach and nearly walked over him. The man leaped backward, his suit seeming to follow a second later.

Wolf apologized.

"Quite all right," the man said. "Yes, Gardner mentioned you. Mr. Pinks, correct?"

"Pinkas, yes."

"You live on the premises, correct?"

Wolf pointed to his cottage.

"Yes. Well. I didn't mean to startle you. Ham Tallaway." He extended a hand. "Development commission. Just a routine inspection."

Wolf said, "How did you get a key?"

"Why, Bob Gardner gave it to me. I'd have rung the bell, but you don't seem to have one." Tallaway laughed. "I'll just look around and be out of your way." While the two men stood talking, Dempsey hobbled out of the cottage and nudged against Wolf's shin. "What a nice kitty." Tallaway bent to pat him. "This retaining wall—you know if it's furrow-grounded, or overlaid?"

Wolf shrugged. "It was here when I arrive."

"I see. Well. Don't let me interrupt you. I'll be done in a few minutes."

When Wolf returned to the cottage, Dempsey was gone. A week later he found the body sprawled beneath a gorse bush just beyond the rear gate. Coal glanced at the frozen eyes and matted fur, then scampered back to the cottage.

With his garden and the new varieties of dehydrated foods, Wolf no longer left the yard more than a few times a year, and then only to cash his checks. His hair grew wild. At rush hour, cars chuffed past, exhaling smog. Ambulances flashed and shrieked, planes roared overhead, black boys loped by on foot, carrying plastic boxes that pumped out cruel imitations of music. Even the quietest moments resounded with electronic beeps and metallic sighs, a faint persistent ringing.

Against these, Wolf placed his wooden shutters and the chirping of tinder in his stove, the music from his phonograph. He allowed ivy to overrun the front gate and found comfort in the gradual vanishing of highway and streetlight and wire. He removed the mailbox and, excepting his monthly stipend, fed to his stove the envelopes dropped near the yard's entrance. He surrendered his battle against the graffiti. Then, without so much as a letter to young Gardner, he bolted the yard shut with a large padlock.

He had hoped to make the ruin outside his kingdom disappear.

But rather than feeling reassured, he felt oddly besieged. His sleep grew restless with dreams.

Wolf had never before remembered his dreams. He might awaken with a strange sense of elation, or dread, even expectation. But as he swung his legs over the edge of his cot, as he sipped his morning tea and surveyed the yard, the turbulent rhythm of these feelings dissipated. He simply immersed himself in the day's routine. As if by a gentleman's agreement, all was forgotten.

Now he woke with distinct memories: a vulture swooping down on Coal while Wolf watched from the doorway of his cottage, unable to wrestle himself into motion. Other nights, Wolf found himself cast out, stumbling through a featureless landscape: the stink of diesel and dead horses, eyes peering at him from dank basements, blue-black air.

Most disturbing was his dream of sleep. He could see himself in this dream. He slept on his mother's deathbed. Yet he could also see images from his childhood: families marched down muddy roads, his father heaped on a wet road, his sisters crying out for potatoes. Bombs dropped from the sky and turned gardens to violent dirt. The dry pop of machine guns shoved bodies into pits. Ashes settled onto his skin. Wolf saw and heard and smelled all of it. Yet he slept. Even as he rose to fire the stove, fifty years on, he could see himself curled peacefully. He looked dead, but he was dreaming.

One day, in the midst of mending a fissured tombstone, Wolf heard the strokes of a hacksaw. He found Ham Tallaway on the other side of the gate. Next to him stood a black man in a work shirt beginning to sweat through.

Tallaway stared at Wolf. "If you wouldn't mind opening the gate, Mr. Pinkas."

"Of course."

"You mean this son of a bitch had the key all along?" The black man scowled. "I been coming out here for how many months, Mr. Tallaway?"

With a strained smile, Tallaway instructed his workman to return to the truck. Wolf swung the gate open and Tallaway proceeded to the nearest shaded bench and sat. "We need to speak, Mr. Pinkas. I am sorry about my colleague, but you can understand his frustration. I myself have grown . . . frustrated. Mr. Gardner has sent a number of letters informing you of the situation, as has the city." He gestured with his chin toward the beheaded mailbox post and paused. "I understand that you have grown quite attached to your home. I see by your care of the premises that you have been diligent in the exercise of your duties. But the city owns this land now. Do you understand?"

"Yes," Wolf said. "I understand." He felt eager to return to his repair, fearful the grout would dry improperly.

Tallaway pulled a handkerchief from his pocket and dabbed his forehead. "And the situation calls for me, you see, to inform you that the city, as it should arise, no longer requires your services."

"Services?"

"It's nothing personal, Mr. Pinkas. We appreciate your dedication," Tallaway said. "This has nothing to do with job performance."

"What you will do? Hire another man?" His tongue flustered at the words.

"No. You see, this property, the city plans to build an arena here. For sports, music concerts, *cultural* events."

"But this is a graveyard. You can't move graves."

"The interred and all existing markers will be relocated," Tallaway said. He folded his handkerchief and tucked it back into his pocket. "Construction won't start until after Christmas, so you have several months to wind up your affairs here. I've discussed the possibility of your obtaining employment with one of our municipal cemeteries. That's a decision for you to make on your own, of course." Tallaway stood and walked to the gate. "I'm sorry," he said without slowing.

That night, Wolf heard a commotion behind his cottage. He

felt certain the dead had been agitated by Tallaway's visit. But the voices were young. They licked the night with laughter. Wolf rose from the cot and fetched his trash stick and his lantern and stepped into the night. Summer, with its languid breath, was gone, but autumn had yet to arrive. A fragment of moon hung in the sky.

The giggling came from the north corner of the yard. Wolf walked past the privy and the brass monument honoring the yard's wealthiest family, past the small clearing where Dempsey had hunted mice, and toward a low wooden gate. Inside, weeds obscured two rows of waist-high headstones. When he first took the job, Wolf tended to the children's graveyard. But these visits became more than he could bear: to be stared at by the mounted photos, forced to consider the bodies below.

Gooseflesh prickled his arms. He heard a cry and stepped inside the gate and made his way toward the back, where two figures were intertwined beneath a stand of cedar. They seemed to be wrestling. He stepped closer and lifted his lantern. For a long moment he watched the boy's muscled back, watched him struggle with the pleasures of congress, arching and thrusting, grunting in satisfaction while the second figure breathed extravagantly and dug her plump ankles into the ropy muscles of her lover's calves. Against the crisp white of the cedar trunks they composed a tableau of brutal desire.

Wolf stepped backward, but in so doing stumbled on a root. The girl lifted her head and looked at him and shrieked. The boy continued his exertions. But she shrieked again and he tumbled from her and they both lay stunned on the blanket they had set down. Bits of dried leaves clung to the girl's braided hair. She ducked behind the boy, who raised his arms as a boxer might and peered into the dull nimbus of Wolf's lantern. "Who the fuck out there?"

Wolf could smell what they had been doing, the slightly putrid scent of bodies opened in this way. The girl reached to cover herself.

"I am the caretaker here," Wolf announced unhappily.

"He's crazy," the girl said. "Look at him, D. Keep him away from me."

The boy reached past her, for his clothes. "Come any closer and I'll kill your ass." He showed his teeth. "I got a gun."

They spoke too fast for Wolf to understand every word. But he saw their fright. "I do not want to hurt you," he said.

"Ain't nobody scared," the boy said. "You the one should be scared."

"This is private property," Wolf said. "A graveyard is here. This is not a place for what you do."

"Look at his face," the girl cried. "*Do* something, D." She squirmed into her T-shirt.

"You have no rights to be here," Wolf said.

The boy seemed to consider this. He took note of the steel-tipped stick in Wolf's hand.

"This ain't no private property," the girl said suddenly. "City own it. We got the same right here as you."

As she spoke, the boy snatched up a pint bottle and dashed away. The girl scrambled after him. They retreated quick and sleek, as if they belonged to the night. Wolf hurried back to his cottage and lay down to calm himself. Wind whistled thinly through the graves. His cottage moaned.

Toward dawn there was a faint knock at the door. Coal lifted his head. Wolf stoked the fire and pulled on his trousers. He rubbed his eyes. As he set the kettle for tea, a second, more distinct knock sounded.

Wolf opened the door. The girl fell to the floor like a swimmer frozen in mid-stroke. Scratches raked the length of her forearms and blood from a gash at the knee ribboned her calf. Her T-shirt rode up around her hips, revealing the muddied seat of her panties. She looked at Wolf and began at once to sob. Wolf thought, for just a moment, of the dying girl he had come upon in a field so many years ago, and of her final wish, at which he shuddered.

"What's happened to you?" Wolf asked. "Was it the boy who did this?"

"Your damn wall too high."

Wolf flew into a brief panic. He wanted the girl gone, out of his home. "There is a place here for washing," he said. "You may clean up. Then you return home. The front gate is open."

The girl nodded drowsily.

When Wolf returned at lunch, he found her on his cot, wearing one of his undershirts, her dirty T-shirt folded and set in a corner. Coal was draped on the prominent swell of her belly. With no great interest, she was inspecting one of his records.

"Young lady," he said.

"You ain't got to tell me," she said. "I was just waiting around to say thanks."

"Yes. I appreciate."

"I'm going," she said. And yet she did not move from the cot.

Wolf looked at her face. Her small features lacked sharpness. She was young. Thirteen? Fourteen?

"I could sue you," she said. "For reckless abuse and some other shit."

Wolf thought about his cache of twenty-dollar bills. Would she have had the ingenuity to check the tin hidden behind his phonograph? "Young lady."

She stood. Coal tumbled and hit the floor with a squeak. Wolf held the door open. But rather than leaving, she ambled around the cottage, inspecting his domestic arrangements, as if he were the interloper and his presence an inconvenience she had chosen, for the moment, to tolerate. "Where you from?" she said.

"What do you mean?"

"You got a accent," she said.

Wolf shook his head. "What does this matter?"

"It don't. I'm just asking."

"You must leave."

"I *am* leaving." She smiled flirtatiously. "You from Mexico?"

"Poland," Wolf said softly.

"You don't look Polish. Them Polish are *big*. Where's your wife, anyway? You old enough to have a wife."

"You must leave," Wolf repeated. "Your mother will worry."

"If you had a wife she'd make you cut that hair, I tell you that right now. Hoo boy, you like one of them flower children. How old are you? You sixty?" She walked over to the stove and peeked inside. "Why you live here? It's *spooky* round here."

Wolf cleared a strand of hair from his face and noted, with some distress, that she was the same height as him. "The front gate is open. Go home. Your mother will worry."

"I live with my auntie. You got any Coke?"

"Young lady—"

"Any kind of *soda*?"

"Young lady," Wolf repeated, as firmly as his manner allowed. "This is my home. I am a busy man."

"Taking care of dead folks. Real busy."

Wolf's cheeks reddened.

"All right, all right. I'm going. Don't get all crazy on me." She looked him up and down, a girl staring out from the body of a woman. Then she began undoing the buttons on her shirtfront.

For a moment Wolf could only watch in astonishment. "That is not necessary. No, please. Stop that, young lady. You may keep that. As, as payment. For your fall."

The girl looked down at the shirt, then over to her T-shirt in the corner. "Fine. You can keep mine, then." She made her way slowly to the door, looking about distractedly. "Your cat's pregnant," she said, before stepping outside.

"What?"

"Your kitty. She pregnant."

"No," Wolf said. "Coal is a boy cat."

"Look at her. She fat. She *pregnant*."

Wolf sighed. "If you need bus fare—"

"Nah." She breezed out. "I don't want nothing from you."

"Do not come back," Wolf called to her. "I am warning."

That night Wolf smelled her everywhere, on his clothes and

on Coal and especially on his cot, a smell like the oil applied to babies. He settled down and cranked his phonograph and attempted to clear his mind for sleep. But the odor interfered. He felt a longing that was not lust, but something less easily dispelled. He wanted to cry out. Coal, lying on the foot of the cot, regarded him quizzically. Wolf rushed outside in his bed shirt. He stumbled this way and that, peering at nothing, at the heavy ink of night, at his garden, at what might have been her footsteps in the dust.

A week later she was back, her voice circling the treetops, then a deeper tone, that of a boy. Wolf selected a record from his collection, an obscure chorale by Emanuel Bach, and cranked his phonograph and listened to Moses sing in German. The cottage swelled with his somber promises, an end to the desert, the milk of Canaan. Wolf closed his eyes and saw her body, bent to its awful purposes.

The next morning he marched to the children's graveyard and stood between the two rows of headstones. The couple had left behind their thin quilt. He burned it in his stove. He drank his tea and struggled to forget these interruptions. But she made this impossible, for she returned to the yard, routinely, on the very night he managed to convince himself he was free of her.

Only in October, with the rains now steady, did her visits cease. As if to compensate, surveyors sent by Tallaway arrived and spent the afternoons pacing the yard's perimeter. A helicopter hovered overhead one morning. Wolf surrendered the pleasures of peaceful sleep. The snows began. He lost track of the days. A notice arrived informing him of the yard's closure. He had thirty days to vacate. Wolf began harboring the conscious wish that he were no longer alive.

On a frigid night deep into December, the girl's voice roused him. He took her screams to be those of ecstasy. Then they lengthened and rose in timbre.

He burrowed under his blankets, for a moment unable to determine if he was awake or asleep, if he lay in the garden of his boyhood or the graveyard that had been his home for thirty years. Then Coal purred thickly, and the phonograph crackled as its needle dipped into the empty grooves at the end of a record. He had been dreaming. A dream.

The girl's next cry drowned out everything. It was like a siren. Wolf threw his coat on over his nightshirt and pulled on his boots. The spirits jeered him. They turned themselves into black veils and twirled indignantly.

He found her in the children's cemetery, on the ground, her legs thrown open. Her monstrous belly heaved under a glaze of sweat. Steamed puffed from between her legs. Her arms lay to each side, like sticks propped in the pegs of her shoulders. Every few seconds her fists pounded the frozen earth. "Oh God," Wolf said. "Young lady. No. No. God, we got to get you to a hospital." He wondered if he might be able to lift her into his wheelbarrow. But she grew panicky when he tried to move her. She wasn't going anywhere.

Wolf felt an instant revulsion at the prospect of having to play a part in the delivery. He told the girl he was going to find help, and started toward the gate. Surely someone had a phone, which would lead to an ambulance, a doctor. But he could hear her pleadings. "Don't leave me! I'm gonna die!" Wolf made it as far as his cottage, then turned back with an armful of blankets. He laid these under her and over her torso. He shucked his coat to make a pillow for her head. There was no choice now—he lowered himself between her legs. The smell of blood and waste punched into the air. Her genitals were red and grotesquely swollen. He reared back and pressed tentatively at her stomach and told her to push. The girl thrashed. She clamped his wrist until the bone ached.

"Push," Wolf said. "You must push." The girl cursed him. "Push," Wolf commanded. "Young lady, please." Wolf could feel the muscles inside her clenching. The baby dropped down into the birth canal. The girl's stomach hardened and her hips bucked and the flesh at her center, engorged with blood, prepared to rend. Snow began to fall. The flakes melted on her legs and Wolf's own reddened hands. "Please," he said. "Young lady, *please*." The girl seized up, let out a wheeze, then ceased moving. Her muscles went slack.

Wolf took off his nightshirt and held it out, as if its presence might coax the child. Naked but for his boots, he entreated the girl. The tears on his cheeks had begun to freeze. Then the idea struck him that the child was asleep. Wolf himself had slept through the trauma of his own birth according to his father. "Your own mother dying and you slept, Wolfie. Peaceful. Asleep."

But if the baby was asleep, and the mother as well, how was the birth to occur? He jostled the girl, to no effect. He kneaded her stomach. Finally his hand came forward and probed unsteadily. It was not like touching earth, the wet rubber of her, the slick hairs, the muck. His fingers slipped inside and immediately felt the baby's head. Her flesh held to it like the seal on a jar of preserves. He pushed in farther and felt something hard against the baby. One of its shoulders was lodged behind the pelvic bone. With a sharp jab Wolf wedged two fingers between the mother and child and tried to pry the child free. Blood and fluid spurted onto his hands. The girl convulsed. He lost purchase.

For a moment, the situation appeared almost comical: he, a naked old hermit crouched in the cold, reaching into a young girl, trying to deliver life into a world he wished mostly to leave. Again he worked his fingers in and searched for the point of contact. He dug at the child's soft shoulder, his fingers cramped. The girl convulsed again and Wolf felt something give, collapse downward.

The baby's head emerged, a dark crescent, then a bit more, a forehead and nose smashed nearly flat. A second dark blotch eased into view, a shoulder, and in a single precarious moment the baby slid out, as if sprung from a trap. Wolf held the steaming body in his huge hands. It dripped and pawed the air, the umbilical cord dangling. He smacked its bottom twice, then a third time, until he heard a sputter. Next, he swaddled the baby in his nightshirt and set it on the mother's chest, nestled beneath the blankets. "Hold," he said, placing her hands on the baby. He shoved one arm under the girl's back and the other under her knees. But she was dead weight now, half-conscious if that. Using his nightshirt as a sling, he tied the baby to his chest and dragged its mother, yard by yard, away from the cedars. The snow fell harder. His knees ached. Blood rushed to the surface of his skin.

Back at the cottage Wolf placed mother and baby on the mattress removed from his cot. He moved the heater close and fed the stove the last of the kindling. With a jackknife he cut through the umbilical cord and moved the baby, a boy, onto his mother's breast. His delicate lips rooted for a nipple, found it, suckled. Wolf boiled water and cleaned the baby as best he could with a towel, then the girl, too. He placed tea bags between her legs to ease the swelling. Coal wandered over and licked at the blood on the stone floor.

Wolf pulled on his trousers and coat and ran outside to fetch wood. He was gone less than a minute. When he returned, he found the baby sprawled beside his mother on the mattress. Coal had retreated to the corner, his tail puffed. Wolf lifted the child and pressed him again to his mother's breast. The child fell away, limp. His eyes were open but clouded. Wolf touched two fingers to his neck and felt a flickering pulse.

He looked at the girl. "What happened here?"

She smiled the glassy smile of delirium. "You killed my baby."

Wolf shook his head. "Something happened to this child."

"You killed him. You a killer."

"No," he whispered. He picked up the child and cradled him against his chest. "I tried to save. Do you understand? I am doing what I can."

She stared blankly at the space where he stood; her eyelids slid down.

"What else must I do? You should have gone to a hospital. Why did you come here? *Why*? I did not ask for you. Why did you bring this trouble into my home?" He looked down at the baby and trembled. "I will not take blame for this, young lady." He knelt and whispered into the girl's ear. "I am trying to save both of you."

But the girl couldn't hear him.

Wolf turned away and struck his head against the stone wall. The baby was still against him, a tiny pulsing thing, and the girl was there, her feverish body tossing. He sank to his knees, re-membering the sting of death, how it left its imprint on even the simplest human gestures. His father set flowers on the dark soil of a grave mound. His sisters—in pinafores and terrified smiles—sang him to sleep. And later, when the war was over and the killing had stopped, he staggered alone into a field and came upon a naked girl, perhaps thirteen, who stared at him from the place where she would perish, whispering her terrible wish. She wanted to be held.

Death did this. It transmuted each act of love into something unbearable. Was it any wonder he had buried himself?

Light seeped through the shutters. Wolf rose from the floor with the baby. He hurried to the door of his cottage and, in one curiously exuberant motion, burst outside. He moved with the child through the cemetery on an old man's legs, aching but stubbornly alive, not seeing the graves he had tended, the head-stones touched with dew, the spirits in their tattered gowns, only hurtling himself toward the gate, the city beyond, a hospital, a doctor, the pink thread of dawn.

ACKNOWLEDGMENTS

Thanks beyond measure to all who read early drafts: Erin Almond, Keith Morris, Billy Giraldi, Tom DeMarchi, Karl Iagnemma, Dave Blair, Victor Cruz, and Pat Flood. To the talented and dependably underappreciated editors who guided these suckers into print: Michael Griffith, James Olney, Rob Spillman, Jodee Stanley, Jeanne Leiby, Andrew Snee, Colleen Donfield, Carolyn Kuebler, Stephen Donadio, Ted Genoways, Michael Martin, and whoever I'm forgetting because I'm an idiot. To the brave and tireless team at Lookout, especially Emily Smith and Ben George, an editor feverish in his desire to set the world afire with words. His attention to the work was miraculous, inspiring, and utterly exhausting. It was an honor to be held to the high standard of your belief, brother.

Lookout Books

LOOKOUT IS MORE THAN A NAME—
it's our publishing philosophy. Founded as
the literary book imprint of the Department
of Creative Writing at the University of North
Carolina Wilmington, Lookout pledges to seek
out emerging and historically underrepresented
voices, as well as works by established writers
overlooked by commercial houses. In a
publishing landscape increasingly indifferent
to literary innovation, Lookout offers a haven
for books that matter.

TEXT WARNOCK PRO 10.5 / 14
DISPLAY CHARCOAL CY 14